Whirlwind

Whirlwind

❧ ❧ ❧

ALISON HART

LAUREL-LEAF BOOKS

Copyright © 2010 by Alison Hart
All rights reserved. Published in the United States by Laurel-Leaf,
an imprint of Random House Children's Books, a division of
Random House, Inc., New York.

Laurel-Leaf Books with the colophon is a registered trademark of
Random House, Inc.

Visit us on the Web! www.randomhouse.com/teens

Educators and librarians, for a variety of teaching tools, visit us at
www.randomhouse.com/teachers

Library of Congress Cataloging-in-Publication Data
Hart, Alison.
Whirlwind / by Alison Hart.
p. cm.
Sequel to: Shadow horse
Summary: While working at Second Chance Farm, a rescue center,
Jas tries to find Whirlwind, her favorite horse that she thought had
been killed by its wealthy and unscrupulous owner.
ISBN 978-0-375-86005-8 (pbk.) —ISBN 978-0-375-96008-6 (lib. bdg.)
ISBN 978-0-375-86006-5 (e-book)
[1. Horses—Fiction. 2. Animal rescue—Fiction.
3. Mystery and detective stories.] I. Title.
PZ7.H256272Wh 2010
[Fic]—dc22
2009016491

Printed in the United States of America
10 9 8 7 6 5 4 3 2 1
First Edition

*This book is dedicated to all those
who use their time and energy to foster and
advocate for animals and children.*

Whirlwind

Prologue

✤   ✤   ✤

June

Jasmine slid the hoof pick into her back pocket, picked up the grooming box, and headed for Whirlwind's stall. It was later than usual—she'd had a ton of homework—but she wanted to ride before dinner.

She hurried down the aisle of the barn. Whirlwind wasn't in her stall, so Jas grabbed a lead line and headed for the mare's paddock. She waved to her grandfather, who was trimming bushes around the Robicheaux mansion.

Jas whistled for Whirlwind, surprised when there was no answering whinny. Even weirder, she didn't see the mare at all.

An ugly thought filled her. Had Hugh Robicheaux sold Whirlwind without telling her? The mare had gotten a lot of attention at the Devon Horse Show. Money ruled Hugh's decisions. If the price was right, he wouldn't hesitate to sell Jas's favorite horse. Even if it broke her heart.

"Whirlwind?" Jas called as she hurried toward the paddock. By now, the mare should be hanging her head over the fence, whickering furiously.

Something was wrong.

Jas broke into a run. She spotted the mare, lying on her side in the middle of the paddock; one eye was open, staring emptily at the sky.

"Grandfather!" Jas hollered. Dropping the grooming box, she slammed open the gate and ran to the downed horse. "It's Whirlwind!"

Falling to her knees, Jas laid her palm against the mare's neck. It felt cold. Hugh and Grandfather came running.

"Hurry!" she screamed. "Something's horribly wrong!"

Grandfather bent and checked the mare's pulse under the lower jaw. His face fell. "I'm so sorry," he whispered.

Tears streamed down Jas's cheeks. "I don't understand. How . . . ?"

"This is how." Stooping, Hugh picked up an evergreen branch. "It's yew. What's this doing in the paddock, Karl?" he demanded. "Do you have an explanation?"

Slowly, Jas's grandfather stood up. "No, Mr. Robicheaux. I don't. I know how poisonous yew is."

"You were the only one trimming the hedges this morning."

"Sir, I'd never be so careless. You can't blame me for killing Whirlwind."

"Who else could have done it?" Hugh's accusing glare swung to Jas.

Startled, she swiped away her tears. "No, sir, it wasn't Ja—" Suddenly, Grandfather clutched his head. His face twisted with pain.

"Grandfather?" Jas awkwardly caught him as he slumped to the ground. Kneeling beside him, she grabbed his hand. "What's wrong?"

Hugh whipped out his cell phone. "I'm calling the police."

Jas looked up at him, stunned. "The police?"

"I have a dead horse here, thanks to your grandfather."

"You can't be serious." She gaped at him. "You know he didn't kill Whirlwind!"

"The evidence speaks for itself."

As Hugh put the cell phone to his ear, his

gaze slid toward Jas, and she saw a glint in his eyes. The same glint she'd seen when he had sold a $50,000 filly for $100,000. The same glint when the favored rival at Devon suddenly went lame.

She sprang to her feet. "You did this."

"Oh, really?" He arched one brow, his attention shifting to the phone. "Hello. I have a police emergency."

Fury replaced Jas's tears. "You killed Whirlwind." With trembling fingers, she yanked the hoof pick from her back pocket. "And you're not getting away with it by blaming my grandfather!" Holding the pick like a weapon, the curved point aimed at Hugh's face, Jas lunged.

One

✣   ✣   ✣

August

"OW! THAT HURT!" JASMINE SCHULER SCOLDED the huge chestnut horse she was grooming. Shadow pricked his ears gleefully. Quickly Jas curled her fingers into pretend teeth. When Shadow swung around to nip her again, she "bit" him on the side of his mouth.

Throwing up his head, the gelding stared at her in surprise.

Jas stifled a laugh. Shadow was special, because she'd helped rescue him from a killer auction. He'd had an untreated thyroid condition and had been in bad shape. Now that the horse was healthy, he'd turned into a brat who needed to learn proper manners.

Shadow inspected his feed tub, licking it

for leftover grain instead of trying to bite her again. "That's better," Jas praised.

When Shadow had arrived at Second Chance Farm, an animal rescue facility, Jas had turned him out with Jinx, a quiet quarter horse. Jinx used flattened ears and his teeth to put the bigger gelding in his place. Jas was trying to do the same, and it was starting to work.

As a reward for good behavior, she massaged the crest of his neck. *Horse massage.* Jas had been riding from the time she could walk. Yet, since living at the rescue farm, her foster home, she'd learned so many new things about animals.

While Jas brushed Shadow's springy mane, she thought about how her life had changed. Less than two months ago, she'd been living at High Meadows, a premier horse farm. Her grandfather, Karl, was the resident caretaker. She had worked there, too, grooming and riding the farm's top-rated show horses. Then the owner, Hugh Robicheaux, had accused Grandfather of killing Jas's favorite horse, a beautiful chestnut Thoroughbred named Whirlwind. Grandfather had been so distraught that he'd had a stroke. He'd gone to the hospital, then a nursing home. Jas had been so angry she'd attacked Hugh. She'd ended up in court, then in foster care.

Foster care. Jas yanked at a tangle in Shadow's mane. When she'd first arrived at Second Chance Farm, she'd been miserable. Now she loved it here. But soon her grandfather was getting out of the nursing home. Foster care would end. Originally, her social worker had arranged for Jas and Grandfather to live in an apartment, which meant that Jas wouldn't be able to take care of Shadow. Miss Hahn, her foster mom, had arranged for the big horse to be adopted.

Even now, Jas's heart twisted at the thought of losing Shadow. And not just because she'd lost so much already. She *loved* the giant goof of a horse.

But at the last minute, Miss Hahn had decided against adopting out Shadow. She had asked Jas and Grandfather to live with her at the farm. Jas would continue caring for Shadow and the other animals, and Grandfather would work as a caretaker. It was a second chance for both of them.

Jas hugged Shadow, her arms barely reaching around his huge neck. "You're still mine to love," she told him. *So why am I not totally happy?*

Whirlwind. Jas slid the worn photo from the back pocket of her jeans. The mare's head was high, her ears pricked for the camera. A tricolored ribbon hung from her bridle. Jas sat in the saddle, posing for the camera, too. Her expression was triumphant, *sparkling.* The picture had been taken last May after they'd won a championship at Devon.

Now the mare was gone.

A chorus of honking and clucking announced the arrival of Miss Hahn. Jas stuck the photo back in her pocket. She peered from the stall just as her foster mother strode into the barn, her stiff leg swinging. Trotting after her was an entourage of animals: geese, cats, and chickens. Jas had nicknamed them "the underfoot gang," because they always got in the way. Old Sam, a German shepherd, and Rose, the farm's potbellied pig, had been patiently waiting for Jas outside Shadow's stall. But when they spotted Miss Hahn, they rushed toward her, tails wagging furiously.

"They're like paparazzi stampeding a celebrity," Jas said to her foster mother. "All you need is a red carpet and evening gown instead of a dirt floor and overalls." Her light mood faded when she saw the solemn look on Miss Hahn's face.

"Officer Lacey from Animal Control called. We have an emergency," Miss Hahn said. "The trailer's hitched and ready. Chase isn't here yet, and I'd like some help. You still have time before lockdown. How about it?"

As part of her sentence for assaulting Hugh, Jas wore a transmitter around her ankle. It kept track of her whereabouts. She wasn't allowed to leave the house except for preset times.

"Um . . ." Jas chewed her bottom lip. While living at the farm, she'd worked with many of the animals that were recovering from abuse. But except for a trip to a horse auction, she'd never been on an actual rescue, although she'd heard the gut-wrenching stories from Chase and the other volunteers.

"It's your choice," Miss Hahn said. "Not everyone has the interest—or the stomach."

"I'll go," Jas said. "Rescuing is important, and I want to help."

"Good. Grab a halter, a lead line, and a bucket of oats. I'll let Officer Lacey know we're on our way." Without waiting for a reply, Miss Hahn strode from the barn.

Jas patted Shadow. "Don't think for a

minute this means no ride today. It'll just have to wait until this afternoon." She gave him one more swipe with the brush, then laid her cheek against his sleek neck. Oh, how she loved this horse. Thank heavens she hadn't lost him, too.

"Jas, I'll meet you in the truck!" Miss Hahn's voice rang from the office trailer. Hastily, Jas picked up the grooming box. When she opened the stall door, Sam leaped to his feet. Rose waddled after her to the supply room, grunting excitedly.

"You're on a diet. Vegetables only, remember?" Jas said as she unbolted the pig-proof latch on the door. Rose squealed, her eyes barely visible in her folds of fat. Ignoring the pig's demands, Jas slipped inside. She grabbed a halter and lead rope and dumped a cup of oats into a bucket. When Jas opened the door again, Rose stomped her stubby legs and cried, "Feed me, feed me, FEED ME!"

Jas sprinkled a few oats on the dirt floor before hurrying from the barn. Mr. Muggins, a new volunteer, was tossing cracked corn to the geese. Earl the rooster strutted around his legs.

Jas waved to Mr. Muggins as she crossed the stable yard. The area around the barns and office was fenced with woven mesh to keep the underfoot gang and other animals safely contained. But the dogs were allowed out the gate. Jas shut it securely behind Sam and wound around the pass-through built into a board fence, which circled the yard and the house. Miss Hahn was waiting in the pickup.

Four more farm dogs met her at the back door of the house. She let all five inside the kitchen, found her baseball cap, and ran to the truck. She stuck the bucket into the truck bed, slid into the passenger's seat, and shut the door. Tucking her light brown hair behind her ears, she put on the cap.

"Here's the situation," Miss Hahn said as she drove down the rutted drive. "Planner's Bank foreclosed on a small farm about five miles from here. The place was owned by a man convicted of making and selling meth. When he landed in jail, his wife couldn't make the mortgage payments. Two weeks ago, she took off. Yesterday the bank's loan officer inspected the property and discovered a horse behind the house. It was in a small paddock with no shelter, food, or water."

Jas blinked in disbelief. "She just left it?"

"Abandoned it without a thought. Like it

was a piece of trash or a sofa. I take that back—she *took* the sofa."

"What condition is it in?"

"Officer Lacey's exact words were 'it brought tears to my eyes,' and he's seen some grim situations."

Jas's stomach knotted. Maybe coming was a mistake.

Miss Hahn turned off the main road onto a dirt lane. "I haven't been back here for years," she said. "Sure is run-down. Though not much worse than our place," she admitted as the truck bumped down the lane, which wound through cedars and locust to a brick ranch house. "Hay prices are sky-high because of the drought. That doesn't leave much for maintenance." She gave a worried sigh. "I'll be glad when your grandfather moves in to help."

She pulled the trailer around a loop and parked under an oak. Jas rolled down the window. The place was eerily silent.

"We must have beat Officer Lacey here," Miss Hahn said. "He's bringing permission from the bank to remove the horse." Draping one arm on the back of the seat, she faced Jas, her mouth set in a line.

"While we're waiting, I have some news." Miss Hahn's gaze darted to the windshield.

Jas tensed. Her foster mother's hesitation signaled one thing: *bad* news.

"Mr. Jenkins called. He's the president of the company that insured Hugh's horses. The company's lawyers are putting together a case against Hugh for insurance fraud. As expected, Hugh's hired a big-name defense lawyer. It's going to be tough to nail him."

Jas gripped the halter, too angry to speak. Whirlwind *was* gone—but Hugh hadn't killed her. The dead horse in the paddock had been a look-alike that Hugh had poisoned. Then he'd claimed it was Whirlwind in order to collect the insurance money.

It had only been a week ago, during an unexpected encounter with Hugh, that Jas had discovered the truth.

Whirlwind's not dead, is she? You killed another horse, a ringer. Then you sold her to someone else.

That's right, Jas. It took me a while to find Whirlwind's twin. But I obviously did a good job, since even you never suspected it wasn't her lying dead in that paddock.

You're evil, Hugh. You may not have killed Whirlwind, but you killed a horse and then made it look like it was Grandfather's fault. And for what?

Money, Jas thought bitterly. The insurance company had paid Hugh $50,000 for a dead horse they thought was Whirlwind.

"Unfortunately, since they have no proof the mare is alive, Mr. Jenkins says the company can't pursue a case against Hugh for Whirlwind," Miss Hahn said, breaking into Jas's thoughts.

"Unless I can find her," Jas said.

A rumble of tires signaled the arrival of Officer Lacey.

"How?" Miss Hahn asked as she opened the truck door. "Hugh's too smart to tell anybody where she is, which means the odds of locating her aren't good. I'm sorry, Jas." Before climbing out of the truck, Miss Hahn asked, "Are you okay?"

Jas nodded, although she *wasn't* okay. That day when she'd been alone with Hugh, he'd confessed that Whirlwind was alive. But it was only her word against his. When the insurance company took him to court, he would admit nothing. That meant she had to find

Whirlwind. Finding her alive would be solid proof that Hugh had committed insurance fraud.

Jas pictured Hugh's arrogant, mocking face. *You'll never find her, Jas. Never.*

"Only I *will* find her," she whispered fiercely. Then a thought made her shiver. Hugh would be determined to keep her from finding Whirlwind. How determined? *Ruthlessly determined.* After all, he'd already murdered two horses.

Two

❖   ❖   ❖

NOT ONLY HAD HUGH KILLED WHIRLWIND'S twin, but he'd also murdered a second horse.

Five years ago, Hugh had killed a horse that was a look-alike for his talented jumper, a Dutch Warmblood named Aladdin, and had collected $30,000 in insurance money. Then he'd sold the real Aladdin for big money. When Aladdin had gotten sick and was no longer able to perform, he'd ended up at a killer auction. That's where Jas had found the skinny, listless horse she'd named Shadow. She had saved him and later discovered he was Aladdin. Now she needed to save Whirlwind.

However, Jas knew the odds of finding the mare weren't good. And Hugh would be determined to stop her. But giving up was *not* an option.

Jas bolted from the truck, her heart pounding. She caught up to Miss Hahn and Officer Lacey as they walked around the house to the trash-littered backyard. A tumbledown garage, its open double doors sagging, was the lone building behind the house. She followed them to a dirt pen fenced in by rusted barbed wire and stacked packing crates.

An animal stood in the middle of the pen. Jas stared, not sure if it was a horse or simply the skeleton of a horse. Its hip bones, spine, and ribs seemed held together only by its hide.

"I don't know how long it's been without food and water," Officer Lacey said. "But the poor thing has eaten the bark off every tree and started peeling wood from the crates."

At the sound of his voice, the horse turned its head. It was covered with sores. Flies rose from its body in a black, buzzing cloud.

"Oh, sweet heaven," Miss Hahn murmured.

Bile rose in Jas's throat. She thrust the halter at Miss Hahn. Clapping her hand over her mouth, she ran to the front of the garage. She grimaced, glad that Chase hadn't come along. He'd be razzing her big-time about being so squeamish.

Jas vowed that this time she *would* handle

it. Dropping her hands, she took deep breaths. Her stomach quit churning. Behind her, something rattled. She peered into the garage, but it was too dark to see. Again she heard the sound. *A skunk? Raccoon?*

Whatever it was, it was dragging something metal—like a chain. She peered closer and heard a whimper.

A dog. Whirling, Jas ran to the truck. Reaching through the open window, she pulled a flashlight from the glove box and raced back. Several feet from the garage, she slowed. If it was a dog, she didn't want to scare it to death. Flicking on the light, she shined it toward the back.

The beam bounced off a small shaggy dog, which trembled from head to tail. "Oh, sweet heaven," Jas repeated Miss Hahn's words. The family hadn't just abandoned a horse.

Jas stepped into the shadows. A chain large enough to hold a Great Dane was attached to the dog's neck. An empty bowl sat beside it. Another chain and empty bowl lay in the dirt as if a second dog had once been tied there. The whole place stunk.

Jas crouched. Maybe if she made herself smaller, the dog wouldn't be so frightened.

"Hello," she said softly. The dog glanced away, submissive.

"Will you let me take the chain off your neck? Would you like some water?" She duck-walked closer and was encouraged when the dog didn't crawl away. "I bet you'd like to come with me to Second Chance Farm. There you'd have plenty of food and friends. The farm helped me when I was all alone." She reached out her hand, but the dog slunk away. Sitting back on her heels, Jas patiently waited. As she gave it time to get used to her, her mind drifted.

When she first thought that Hugh had killed Whirlwind, she'd been lost in anger. It had taken her weeks to trust anyone at her new foster home. She had finally learned to trust Chase, a volunteer who was about her age. He'd helped her figure out the insurance scam that Hugh had pulled, when he'd switched the look-alike with Aladdin. Fortunately, they'd dug up enough evidence so at least the lawyers were charging Hugh with one count of fraud. Now, if she could only find—

A wet tongue licked Jas's knuckles. Startled, she glanced down. The little dog had crawled beside her. It pressed itself against her knee as if desperate for her touch.

Gently she stroked its back, the fur tangled and gritty. Its tail thumped. "So you've decided to trust me?" Her fingers found the chain, which had rubbed its neck raw. "I can't believe someone did this to you." She undid the chain and let it drop. Only she *did* believe it. Hugh had shown her how cruel people could be to animals.

Moving slowly, Jas wrapped her arms around the dog and held its quivering body to her chest. When she stood and walked into the sunlight, it hid its muzzle in the crook of her arm.

She carried it around the garage to the makeshift paddock. Miss Hahn was smearing something on the horse's sores. Officer Lacey was feeding him a handful of hay. Jas was glad to see him chewing hungrily.

She'd learned that an animal suffering from malnutrition had to be gradually reintroduced to food. Starvation messed up the animal's digestive system. Horses given too much feed too fast could colic, founder, or die. "How's he doing?" she asked.

"He's young," Miss Hahn said. "So I think he'll be okay. What's that you're holding?"

"A dog I found tied in the garage." Jas wrinkled her nose. "It's filthy, skinny, and scared."

"Officer Lacey," Miss Hahn said. "Do we need the bank's permission to take an abandoned dog to Second Chance Farm?"

"What dog?" the officer asked, winking at Jas.

Miss Hahn smiled. "You've fifteen minutes to lockdown, Jas. Perhaps Officer Lacey can drop you back at the farm. Chase can help with the dog. He'll know what to do."

Jas rolled her eyes. *Of course Chase will.* "What about loading the horse in the trailer?"

"I called Rand. He's coming over. I called Dr. Danvers as well. He's coming to the farm this evening to check the colt."

"Good, he can take a look at this stinky critter, too. And before you leave, will you make sure there's not another dog?" Jas asked. "This one had a chain around its neck. There's a second chain but no animal."

"I will. Now scoot before your lockdown time runs out."

Jas shifted the pile of bones and fur in her arms. The dog was about the size of a small beagle but weighed practically nothing. She followed Officer Lacey to his van. ANIMAL CONTROL was written on its side.

He opened the door and she slid in, holding

the dog carefully. A Plexiglas partition separated the front from the back of the vehicle, which was sectioned into two cages. One side contained a box of dog treats, towels, leather gloves, a cat carrier, a Havahart trap, and a control pole with a noose at the end. Balding and pudgy, Officer Lacey was a genius at coaxing animals, not chasing them.

When they started up the drive, Jas heaved a sigh, glad to leave the creepy place behind. "Any suggestions on how to care for the dog?" Jas asked Officer Lacey. She didn't want Chase to be the only know-it-all.

"Small amounts of dry food, small sips of water. A flea bath. Later it will have to be wormed and vaccinated. For now, keep it separate from the other dogs until Dr. Danvers has checked it out."

"Thanks." When they reached the farm, she gathered the dog in one arm and opened the door.

"May I name it?" Officer Lacey asked before she got out. "I never get to name the rescues and strays. I can't get attached."

"Sure. Then we can quit calling it 'the dog.'" Jas tipped it sideways so she could see under its belly. "Looks like it's a girl."

"I'd like to name it Hope, then," he said. "In hope that she'll have a good life from now on."

Jas smiled. "I like that name. Thanks again."

As Jas climbed from the van, Chase came striding toward her, five dogs on his heels. He wore cutoffs, a T-shirt, an Orioles baseball cap, and an adorable grin. Jas tried to ignore the adorable grin.

Ever since Jas had arrived at the farm, she'd been attracted to Chase. She'd never had a boyfriend before. Horses were her sole focus. She and Chase were just good friends. *And nothing more.* That was the way she wanted to keep it.

Because if she was going to find Whirlwind and defeat Hugh, she couldn't get distracted.

At least that's what she told herself.

Three

❖ ❖ ❖

"MISS HAHN JUST CALLED. YOU FOUND A DOG?"
Chase asked. He was a year older than Jas, but
he already knew that he wanted to be a veterinarian and loved the challenge of a new rescue.

"Her name's Hope. Officer Lacey named
her."

Chase tipped back his cap and inspected
the ball of fur in her arms. The dogs crowded
around, sniffing and wagging their tails. "Does
she have a head?"

Jas laughed. "It's tucked underneath. The
poor thing's scared to death. Probably thinks
she'll be mauled by these five slobbering
mutts."

"We need to feed her a little dry food and
water, then give her a flea bath," Chase instructed
as they walked side by side toward the house.
"We can't afford a flea infestation."

"I know, Chase," she said. "I'm not *stupid*."

"*Really?*" He feigned shock.

Jas would have socked him, but she didn't have a free hand.

Chase opened the door into the kitchen, shooing the other dogs away while Jas went inside. She set Hope by the array of food and water bowls. The pup stood hunched and trembling. "She's got to be hungry," Jas said. But when Chase placed a bowl of kibble on the floor, she only stared mournfully at it.

Fifteen minutes later, after coaxing Hope to eat a few bites, Jas carried her to the laundry room. Chase had gathered shampoo and towels and had filled the deep sink with a few inches of warm water. When Jas set Hope in the sink, the pup scrambled and clawed to get out.

"At least we know she's got some fight left," Jas said, trying to keep the dog in the tub.

Chase picked up the shampoo. "Hold on to her while I squirt some soap on her back."

"Why do I have to hold her? I'm getting soaked."

"Can't you handle a five-pound dog?" He squirted a stream of soap, hitting her arm.

"Can't you handle the soap? You're getting it everywhere but on her." Jas gritted her teeth as Hope struggled. "She didn't move the whole ride here. Now she's a tiny tornado."

"Okay, you do the soap—since you are seriously messing up the holding part." Setting down the bottle, Chase took Hope from her. "She's probably never had a bath before. This will traumatize her for life."

"Thank you, Dr. Chase, dog psychologist." Finally, Hope stopped wiggling long enough for Jas to soap her back. As Jas scrubbed, she told Chase about the skeletal horse and finding Hope. "There was a second chain and bowl in the garage. Miss Hahn's going to look around to see if there's another abandoned dog."

"I say we go back and tie up their so-called owners without any food or water," Chase said.

"For once we totally agree." Jas sprayed Hope with the hose. Dirt poured off as she rinsed, changing the dog's fur from brown to white. "I wonder what breed she is?"

"Mutt." Chase pulled the plug to let out the water. "Like all the dogs at the farm except for Old Sam."

When Hugh had threatened to put down Grandfather's aging German shepherd, Chase and Jas had "dognapped" him from High Meadows Farm.

Jas finished rinsing Hope, careful to keep water out of her eyes and ears. The wet fur clung to the little dog. She could see every rib.

"Dang, she's ugly and skinny," Chase said. "And she's got little scabby things on her. Officer Lacey should have named her Rat."

"Rat? That's disgusting." Jas dried the pup with a towel. "She's shaking. I'll sit with her in the sun on the front porch."

"Are you on lockdown now?" Chase asked, just as he'd asked every day since she'd arrived. At first, Jas swore he couldn't tell time. Then she decided he was simply impatient with her schedule.

"Yeah. I'll be so glad when I get this stupid transmitter off my ankle. Only three more days until my court date. Mr. Petrie, the public defender, thinks the hearing will go in my favor."

"Then you won't be a foster kid anymore," Chase said. "You're still staying here, though, right?" He was washing the mud down the drain, not meeting Jas's eyes, so she knew the answer was important to him.

"Of course. Miss Hahn's looking for a mobile home for Grandfather and me to live in."

"Good." Chase hid his relief by glancing down at the transmitter around her leg. "I'll be glad, too, when the judge lets you remove that thing. Then you can start doing some real work around here instead of sitting on your—"

"I do *plenty*." Jas threw suds at him, which landed on his cap.

"Hey," he protested. "Quit messing with the Orioles."

Wrapping Hope in two towels, Jas lifted her from the sink. "Chase, can you stop joking for one sec?"

"One sec . . ."

"What if Hugh shows up for my hearing?"

"I'll lock him in the men's room."

"I knew you wouldn't take this seriously. Forget I asked." Plucking a dry towel off a shelf, she hurried from the laundry room.

"Slow down." Chase followed her. "Why are you so touchy? You just said the hearing should go in your favor."

"I'm really worried."

"About what?"

She bit her lip and draped the dry towel

over her shoulder, shifting Hope in her arms. "What if Hugh gives the judge the security tape?"

Part of Jas's probation was to never step foot on Hugh's farm again. But Jas and Chase had sneaked into the stable at High Meadows trying to find proof that Shadow was Aladdin. The farm's surveillance camera had caught them on tape. Chase knew about the tape, but he didn't know about Hugh's threats.

I have a great shot of you and your boyfriend sneaking into the barn. How do you think he'll like the juvenile detention center?

"He said he'd use it against me if I didn't keep my mouth shut about Whirlwind," Jas told him. "And he threatened you, too."

For a second, Chase looked startled. "Me?" Then he shrugged. "No big deal. I'll tell my dad about it tonight." Chase's dad was an investigator for the Stanford Police Department.

"You're not worried?"

"There's nothing we can do about it. If Hugh shows up waving the tape and hollering 'arrest those trespassers,' we'll deal with it."

Jas wished she could be as nonchalant as Chase.

"Thanks for worrying about me." He grinned, and his blue eyes met hers. Despite her chilled T-shirt and the wet dog, Jas's insides flared.

"Oh, go fix up that quarantine stall for Hope." Turning abruptly, she hurried across the living room. She didn't want him to see her flushed cheeks.

"Aye, aye, Commandant Schuler." Seconds later, the screen door slammed, and she heard him whistle for the dogs.

Jas carried Hope outside and sat on the front porch swing. She hated to admit it, but Chase was right. There was nothing she could do about the dreaded tape. It wasn't her biggest problem, anyway. Finding Whirlwind was.

Unwrapping the wet towel from around the dog, she replaced it with the dry one. Hope snuggled deep into the folds. The sun was hot and comforting, and Jas settled back against the wood slats. Soon her T-shirt dried, and the pup in her lap stopped shaking. When she peeked under the towel, Hope was asleep.

She gave the swing a push with her foot. *Hope.* Officer Lacey had no idea how perfect that name was. Not just for the dog, but for her, too. Jas was going to need a barn full of hope if she was going to find Whirlwind.

The mare had been gone for two months. She knew the exact day that Hugh must have gotten rid of her—June 1, the day after Phil, the manager of High Meadows Farm, and Grandfather had left for Maryland to pick up cattle. That same day, she'd caught the bus early to get to school for a makeup test. That left Hugh at the farm, *alone,* to set up his devious plan.

Had he shipped Whirlwind overseas or sold her to a buyer in California? Jas had no idea. But with Whirlwind gone, he'd somehow substituted the look-alike mare in her place. A mare he must have starved so she would eat the deadly yew he'd tossed in the paddock after Grandfather returned so that he, not Hugh, could be blamed for the "accidental" poisoning.

The mare had died in pain, her guts twisting. Then all Hugh had to do was claim she was Whirlwind and collect the insurance money.

Jas kicked the swing higher. The man was a monster who had intentionally killed two horses. And if he showed up for her court hearing, that was what Jas would tell the judge. If

Chase wasn't worried about the surveillance tape, she wouldn't be, either.

Tightening her arms around the warm bundle, Jas held Hope close. At her first court hearing, she'd been too afraid of Hugh to talk.

This time she wouldn't keep her mouth shut.

Four

✣　　✣　　✣

"THE COLT HAS A BODY-CONDITION SCORE OF
one-point-five," Dr. Danvers said that evening.
He was inspecting the new rescue horse, which
had been placed in a quarantine stall set apart
from the main barn. Rescue farms had to be
super-careful when bringing in new animals
because of the many contagious diseases and
infections.

Miss Hahn glanced at the clipboard in her
hand. "I assigned him a one-point-five, too."

"A one-point-five is considered bad, right?"
Jas asked. She held the colt's halter as Dr. Danvers prepared a syringe to draw blood.

"A one is the worst. It means extremely
poor," Miss Hahn explained. "An ideal score
for a horse is five."

"Say cheese," Chase said from the doorway. He was shooting photos to document the

horse's condition. They'd be added to the colt's growing folder.

Jas patted the little horse's face. He didn't move when Dr. Danvers stuck him with the needle. She ran her gaze over every inch of his body. His fly-chewed sores were almost worse than his protruding bones.

Dr. Danvers capped the syringe. Pulling a pen from the pocket of his coveralls, he asked, "Got a name yet?"

"Don't let Chase name him," Jas said. "He wanted to call the new dog Rat."

"How about Wonder?" Dr. Danvers suggested. "As in, it's a Wonder he's still alive."

"I like the name," Jas agreed.

"Then Wonder it is." Miss Hahn wrote the name on the folder tab.

"Can you look at Rat—I mean, Hope—next?" Chase asked Dr. Danvers. The dog was quarantined in the stall next door. "She might have mange."

"And Shadow's due for a rabies vaccination," Jas added. "And Ruffles needs his teeth checked."

Miss Hahn laughed as Dr. Danvers nodded patiently. The veterinarian smiled at her, and her sun-brown cheeks turned red.

Chase gave Jas a knowing look. The two were convinced that Miss Hahn and Dr. Danvers were secretly in love with each other. Chase lowered his head. "Did you notice they're wearing matching coveralls?" he whispered out of the side of his mouth, and Jas choked on a laugh.

"What's so funny?" Miss Hahn asked, shooting a suspicious frown their way.

"Chase, being stupid as always," Jas said quickly.

They left Wonder's stall. The colt would be in quarantine for seven days. During that time, a volunteer would be assigned to lavish extra TLC on him. Neglected animals needed mental as well as physical rehabilitation.

One more thing Jas had learned living at the farm.

Dr. Danvers changed gloves before going into Hope's stall. Chase was kneeling next to the dog. She was curled in a ball on a worn, clean blanket. She took one look at the vet and began to tremble.

Gently, Dr. Danvers prodded and probed her eyes, mouth, and body. "No mange. Just flea bites. Sure is skinny."

"We gave her a flea bath this afternoon,"

Chase announced, as if they'd performed major surgery.

Jas pressed her fingers against her lips to hold back another laugh. Still, a snort escaped and he gave her an "I'll get you later" look.

"Meet you at Shadow's stall," Jas told Dr. Danvers before heading from the barn. Although "barn" was an exaggeration, since it was a converted shed. The outside walls were unpainted boards, and the roof was rusted tin. Miss Hahn dreamily talked about a modern, quarantine barn with washable walls and floors, but it required money to make dreams a reality.

Outside the door were a spigot, a bucket, a trash can, a laundry basket, and strong soap. Jas washed her hands carefully, scrubbing under her fingernails. Then she pulled the protective shoe covers off her sneakers and tossed them in the basket.

The quarantine barn was surrounded by wire mesh fencing to keep the other animals safe. Sam waited for Jas by the exit gate. When he spotted her, his tail fanned the air excitedly.

"Hello, Sam," Jas greeted as she opened the gate. The old shepherd pressed his nose against her pant legs and snuffled noisily. "Yes, there's a new dog in town. You'll soon get to meet her."

Shutting the gate, Jas waved at Lucy and Rand. The two volunteers were turning out the horses for the evening. Lucy was sixteen, a soon-to-be high school senior and model gorgeous. Rand was sixty, a rodeo-grizzled, retired bull rider. Lucy had helped Jas and Chase sneak onto High Meadows Farm. Fortunately, she hadn't been captured on the surveillance tape.

Jas hurried to the barn, grabbed a halter and rope, and went into Shadow's stall. He struck the wall with his hoof, anxious to get out. "Cool it." She calmed him with a shoulder massage. "We've got to wait for Dr. Danvers." She hoped Chase wouldn't tag along; she wanted to talk to the vet, alone.

If Jas was ever going to find Whirlwind, she needed more information. Dr. Danvers had been High Meadows Farm's veterinarian when she and Grandfather had lived there. He'd been the one to locate the identification microchip in Shadow's neck that proved he was really Aladdin, and that led to the insurance fraud investigation. Now Jas was hoping that Dr. Danvers had some idea how to find Whirlwind.

"Jas?" She heard Dr. Danvers holler.

"Down here!"

When the veterinarian peered over the stall door, Shadow snorted and backed into the corner. "Quit being such a baby," Jas scolded the gelding. "It's just a shot."

"He looks good," Dr. Danvers said, opening the door. "You were right about his thyroid condition. The supplement has done wonders for his energy and his coat." While the vet talked, he stepped nonchalantly to Shadow's side and stuck the needle in his neck. "Done."

Jas scratched the gelding's chest. "See? That wasn't so bad."

"I'll leave another container before I go."

"Don't forget Ruffles." With Shadow prancing beside her, Jas followed Dr. Danvers down the aisle. "Let me turn this goof out and I'll help you with her."

"No need. Ruffles and I are buddies. Meet me by the truck and I'll give you that supplement."

Jas led Shadow to a large field that he shared with Jinx and two other geldings, Gambler and Cadet. She opened the gate and unbuckled the halter. When it slipped from his muzzle, Shadow wheeled and raced toward the other three horses. All four took off, galloping down the hill. Gambler and Cadet were two-year-old Arabian geldings. They'd been rescued the past winter from a bare feed lot. Jas had seen the "before" photos. Now, after six months, they were plump and glossy.

Seconds later, the four horses raced back. Jinx, Cadet, and Gambler, too hot for a longer chase, dropped their heads to graze. Shadow trotted around them, his tail fanning behind, his chestnut coat glistening in the evening sun.

Jas remembered the first time she'd turned him out. He'd been so listless that she'd called him a plodding old school horse. What a difference.

"Jas!" Dr. Danvers stood at the back of his truck, holding up a plastic container.

She hurried over and took it from him. "Before you go . . ."

"You have some questions?" he guessed.

Jas nodded.

"First, I've got some not-so-good news for you." Dr. Danvers frowned. "I still can't find my old file on Aladdin that listed his microchip number, and . . ." He hesitated. "The clerk from the insurance company is now saying that Shadow's number doesn't match Aladdin's. That they aren't the same horse."

"What?" Jas exclaimed, even though she knew what had happened. *The clerk will say that the company made a mistake.* Hugh had paid them off.

"Let's hope that the National Microchip Registry didn't destroy their records."

"Which should be enough proof, right?"

"That's up to the lawyers."

Frustrated, Jas drummed her fingers on the top of the container. "That means I *really* need to find Whirlwind. She'd be solid proof that Hugh kills horses for money. Only I have no clue where to look. I know that Hugh must have shipped her from High Meadows on June first. After that, I'm stumped. He could have sold her to anyone, anywhere."

Dr. Danvers thought a minute, then said, "Hugh's clients are scattered all over the United States. However, he would probably sell Whirlwind to someone who wouldn't look too closely at the Jockey Club registration. If the horse killed in Whirlwind's place was a Thoroughbred, Whirlwind might be using her registration. Or Hugh could have forged one."

"Either way, Whirlwind would have a different name."

"Right. She didn't have an ID chip like Aladdin. I remember asking Hugh if he wanted me to insert microchips in his horses in case of theft. He scoffed and said he trusted the farm's security system." Dr. Danvers walked to the driver's side and opened the truck door. "I bet he planned this latest scheme a long time ago, after he got away with it with Aladdin. He *wanted* Whirlwind to be impossible to trace."

"*Impossible?*"

"I'm sorry, Jas." He climbed into the truck. She stepped away as he shut the door. "Let's hope the lawyers can nail Hugh for the scam with Shadow," he said out the rolled-down window. "Hey"—he gave her a thumbs-up—"I'll see you at the courthouse on Thursday for your hearing."

"Sure," Jas said, not sure at all. The words *impossible to trace* were pounding too loudly in her head.

"*Yoo-hoo.* Earth to Jas?" A hand flapped in front of her face. Lucy was peering closely at Jas. Her long blond hair was in a neat ponytail, and her lip gloss, foundation, and mascara were photo-shoot ready despite the evening heat.

"We've got stalls to clean," Lucy said, arching one perfectly plucked brow. "You all right? You're white as a ghost."

Quickly, Jas pretended to study her fingers. "No, darn it, I broke a nail. Major trauma."

Lucy snorted through her perky nose. *"Rrright,"* she drawled, glancing at Jas's chewed nails.

She followed Lucy to the barn, half listening as the older girl chattered about riding horses for some rich owner. "I need to make some money before school starts this fall. You know, senior prom, senior pictures . . . Oh, I guess you don't know about all that since you'll be a lowly freshman."

Thanks for reminding me about school, Jas thought sourly.

Stopping, Lucy shouted above the roar of the tractor, which Chase was driving down the aisle. "The lady's paying me twenty bucks a horse. You're not the only equestrienne around here." She propped one fist on her cocked hip and faced Jas. "She's Hugh's neighbor. Does that bother you?"

"Should it?" Jas eyed Lucy. Despite her boasting, Lucy wasn't a great rider, so if some lady was paying her, the woman had to be clueless or desperate.

"Her farm's on Mill Road, near High Meadows. It's called Blissful Acres." Lucy glanced around the barn. "Sure makes this place look like a dump."

Jas bristled, even though she'd thought the same thing when she first arrived. She knew the owner of Blissful Acres, Mrs. Vandevender, whose pudgy horses were basically lawn ornaments.

Turning off the motor, Chase hopped off the tractor, which he'd parked at the end of the aisle. "Are you guys going to do any work?" he asked.

"Not for long," Lucy said. "I'm off to Blissful Acres."

"They won't be blissful once you start riding there," Chase joked, and Jas started laughing.

Lucy gave them both looks of disgust before heading into the supply room. "I guess she didn't think that was funny," Chase told Jas. "What's she talking about, anyway?"

"Lucy's gone to the dark side. She's riding for money."

"Are you surprised?" Chase grabbed the rake and pitchfork, which were leaning against the wall. "After she got a look at fancy High Meadows Farm, it was no turning back for her. Besides, how else is she going to pay for all that makeup she wears?" He held out the pitchfork. "Here, you pitch. I'll rake. Lucy's going to lime."

Jas took the pitchfork and went into the first stall. Chase followed her. "No argument?" he asked. "No reminding Lucy that she limed yesterday so it's your turn?"

"No argument." Jas forked up a hunk of pee-soaked straw. The sharp smell made her nose sting and her eyes water, hiding her threatening tears. How would she find Whirlwind if the mare was *impossible* to trace?

As Chase raked manure into piles, he kept glancing her way. Finally he asked, "What were you and Dr. Danvers talking about before he left?" When she didn't answer, he stopped raking. "No fair, Jas. If I'm going to be arrested because of that surveillance tape, I deserve to know what's going on."

Sighing, Jas leaned on the handle of the pitchfork. "Dr. Danvers said that finding Whirlwind will be impossible."

"So? Dr. Danvers is a vet, not a detective."

Jas stared at him. Chase was right. A detective might be able to track down Whirlwind. And Mr. McClain, Chase's father, was an investigator with the Stanford Police Department. "Do you think your dad . . . ?"

"I can ask him. He knows what's going on. So if we're going to nail Hugh and find Whirlwind, no more secrets. Deal?" His expression was so earnest, Jas had to smile.

"Deal."

He started raking again. When he looked over and caught her still smiling at him, she blushed and braced herself for some major teasing.

But he only smiled, too, and Jas felt her insides flutter. Spinning around, she attacked a pile of manure. Chase was such a great friend. And she had needed a friend when she'd first arrived at Second Chance Farm. More importantly, now she trusted and *needed* him to help her find Whirlwind.

But that didn't mean she was ready to trust him with her heart.

Jas flipped the page in her novel. It was about a girl's infatuation with a vampire, only the girl acted so stupid and *in luv,* Jas couldn't concentrate on the story.

It was Thursday, the day of her hearing. Jas wore a crisp white shirt, a denim skirt, and sandals, hoping to look appropriately repentant when she went before the judge. Still, she nervously twirled a strand of hair.

In front of her, Chase paced the hall of Stanford Municipal Court. Beside her on the bench, Miss Hahn completed paperwork. At the other end, Jas's social worker, Miss Tomlinson, was talking on her cell phone.

Jas glanced at the building's double front doors. Dr. Danvers was bringing Grandfather from the nursing home. *Where are they?*

Her grandfather was important to her case. The judge had to see that he was healthy enough to regain custody of Jas. She loved Miss Hahn, but she was tired of being a foster kid.

"Chase, would you *sit down*?" she whispered, slamming shut her book. "You're making me crazy."

"This waiting is making *me* crazy," he said, continuing to stalk. He wore khakis and a light blue cotton shirt. Jas had never seen him in anything but cutoffs or jeans and T's. The shirt brought out the blue in his eyes, his sun-streaked hair looked silky-soft, and his . . .

Oh, stop it, Jas scolded herself. *You are not a love-struck idiot in a novel.*

She pointed to a closed door down the hall. "At least we're waiting here and not in the holding cell. That's where the deputies brought me for my first hearing." She shuddered, thinking about that day.

"Bender case!" the court bailiff hollered, and Jas jumped. A young kid shuffled from the holding cell, escorted by two deputies. He wore an orange jumpsuit, ankle chains, and handcuffs.

Chase hastily slid onto the bench beside Jas. "Jeez, they've got him chained up like Hannibal Lecter. Hey, they're here." Leaping up, he strode to the double doors and held one open for Grandfather, who hobbled inside using a cane. Dr. Danvers followed behind.

"You made it!" Jas tossed the book on the bench, ran to her grandfather, and wrapped her arms around his wafer-thin frame. A suspender buckle bit into her cheek, but she didn't care. When Jas's mother, Iris, left to pursue her dream of jockeying, Jas's grandparents had raised her. A year ago, her grandmother had died of cancer. Since then, Jas and Grandfather had been a team. She'd missed him terribly.

"You look terrific." She leaned back. His snow-white hair was combed, and his cheeks were razor-smooth.

He rubbed his chin. "Nurse shaved me. Nearly cut off my 'ead." Some of her grandfather's words were slurred because of the stroke, but Jas understood him perfectly.

"Hello, Mr. Schuler." Miss Hahn shook Grandfather's hand. "Jas and I are so excited that you like our plan."

"Plan? What plan?" Grandfather shouted as if deaf, but then he winked. "Don't 'orry, I love the plan. I'm ready to come to your farm and 'ork. Soon I 'on't need 'is." He waved his cane in the air, lost his balance, and would have tipped over if Jas hadn't been holding him. Before the stroke, her grandfather had been able to carry a bale of hay in each hand. Now he could barely walk.

Jas bit the inside of her cheek. *How will he manage living and working at Second Chance Farm?* But she pushed the worry from her mind.

"Jas's case should be called any minute," Miss Tomlinson told everyone. "I expect it to go well. The judge has all the information about the circumstances leading up to her assault on Hugh. The probation officer's and my reports will state that Jas has met her obligations."

Everybody but Jas murmured in relief. Her gut was tangled in a knot. Despite yesterday's bravado, she knew the surveillance tape could screw up everything. She could end up back in foster care with more time on her probation. Chase could be arrested.

The blood rushed from her head. Dizzy, she plopped down on the bench.

"Are you all right?" asked Miss Hahn.

"Put your head between your knees," Dr. Danvers instructed.

Miss Tomlinson opened her purse. "I have smelling salts."

"Get her some 'ater," Grandfather suggested.

"Excuse me." Arm outstretched like a quarterback, Jas sprang from the bench and barreled through them. She raced around the corner. There was a ladies' room in the small commons area, which also had soda and snack machines, an exit door, and a drinking fountain. Ducking her head, she gulped the stream of cool water.

Suddenly, fingers grasped her upper arm, hurling her from the fountain. She slammed against the wall, banging the back of her head.

"Hey—" A palm slapped over her mouth, stifling her cry. Jas twisted and found herself staring straight into Hugh Robicheaux's eyes.

Five

"DON'T SAY A WORD." HUGH GRABBED JAS'S throat with his other hand. "Just listen. You need to stop searching for Whirlwind. She's safe and healthy. Got that?"

How did Hugh know she was looking for Whirlwind?

"Got that?" Hugh tightened his grip, and Jas nodded as best as she could.

"If you persist, you will regret it. I can—and I will—destroy Diane and her precious farm. And as for that boyfriend of yours . . ." He grinned maliciously, his face so close that Jas felt the brush of his foul breath on her cheek. "I doubt he'd want his video debut sent to the police. Right?"

Jas squeaked a "right" beneath his palm.

"I knew you'd agree. Look, I kept my end of the deal. Your grandfather was well cared for at the nursing home. But keep up this fool-ishness, and I'll make sure everyone you love pays dearly. Understand?"

She nodded again.

"Good." Releasing his hold, Hugh spun and pushed open the exit door. Jas gasped, try-ing to catch her breath. Pausing, he glared at her. "Don't forget, I have friends in high places." He tipped his head in the direction of the courtroom. "Not only will I be acquitted of all these foolish insurance fraud charges, but also this meeting better stay between us or you'll regret it."

The door closed behind him. Running out-side, Jas scanned the busy sidewalk and street. He was gone.

She rubbed her neck. She could still feel his fingers, choking her.

"What are you doing out here?" Chase asked. He was holding open the door, looking at her with a puzzled expression.

"I . . . I needed some air." Jas stumbled over the words. Ducking her chin, she tried to pass by him, but he didn't step aside.

"What's wrong with your neck?" He pushed her hair behind her left ear. "It's all red."

She shook her head, afraid to say anything.

This little meeting better stay between us or you'll regret it.

Chase's face darkened. "Hugh was here, wasn't he?" Striding outside, he looked right, then left. When Jas didn't reply, he whirled to face her, his blue eyes snapping. Jas had never seen Chase angry before. "You said no more secrets, Jas, remember?"

"Yes, it was Hugh."

"What did he want?"

"He said if I didn't stop searching for Whirlwind, he was sending the surveillance tape to the police."

"I already told you the tape's no big deal."

"He told me to keep quiet and to stop looking for Whirlwind. How does he know I'm searching for her?"

"He's bluffing."

"He's not bluffing when he said I would regret it if I told anyone he saw me today. And"— her voice rose—"he's not bluffing about having powerful friends and beating the fraud charges against him."

"Jas?" Miss Tomlinson said from the court-house. "They just called your case."

"We're coming," she said, starting inside.

Chase reached for her elbow, holding her

back. "Forget about Hugh for now. You have a lot of supporters here today. Don't let that jerk ruin it."

Nodding quickly, Jas hurried into the courthouse. A deputy in uniform stood outside the courtroom door. Jas joined Grandfather, Miss Hahn, and Dr. Danvers, who were milling in the hall. Miss Tomlinson had already gone in.

Jas flipped up her shirt collar so no one would notice the red marks on her neck. Grandfather put his arm around her shoulders. "It'll be all 'ight," he assured her.

"You may enter." The deputy opened the doors and escorted Jas in first. She gulped nervously when she spotted the robed judge behind his desk in the front of the room. The last time she'd faced him, she'd been convicted of assault.

Slowly, she walked down the aisle between the rows of benches. Mr. Eyler, the probation officer, sat against a wall near the front. He was talking to Miss Tomlinson, who was next to him. Jas's public defender, Mr. Petrie, sat behind the defense table on the right. This time there was no prosecuting attorney at the table on the left.

And no Hugh. Jas's shoulders sagged with

relief as she looked around to make sure. Still, she could feel his presence. *Don't forget, I have friends in high places.* She looked at the judge. He was reading her file, his head bent. Was he Hugh's golfing buddy? Fraternity brother? Distant cousin?

The deputy guided Jas to the chair next to Mr. Petrie. She sat, immediately twisting to look over her shoulder. Miss Hahn, Chase, Grandfather, and Dr. Danvers were seated several rows behind her. They smiled encouragingly. This isn't like the first trial, Jas reminded herself. That time, she'd had no one.

Jas gave them a wavering smile. Then she took a deep breath and faced the judge.

Mr. Petrie was already standing, addressing the bench. "Good morning, Your Honor."

"Good morning, Mr. Petrie," the judge said without looking up from Jas's file.

Jas squirmed in her chair, remembering her trial forty-five days ago.

Miss Schuler, you have been charged with assault against Hugh Robicheaux. Mr. Petrie, how does your client plead?

Your Honor, Miss Schuler pleads not guilty.

Only, she *had* been guilty of attacking Hugh. And she'd do it again today.

Finally the judge looked up from the folder. "I see from the reports that Miss Schuler has met the terms of her probation."

"Yes, Your Honor."

"It is my understanding that Mr. Eyler, Mrs. Weisberger, and Miss Tomlinson have agreed that no further services are necessary for your client."

"That is correct," Mr. Petrie said.

"Is Miss Schuler's grandfather, Karl Schuler, willing and able to cooperate?"

"I am, Your Honor!" Jas heard her grandfather shout.

The judge smiled. "You may sit down, Mr. Schuler. Mr. Petrie will respond for you."

"He is willing and able, Your Honor."

The judge next consulted with the probation officer and social worker. Finally he turned to Jas. "Jasmine Schuler, please stand."

She stood so quickly that the chair scraped the floor with a loud rasp. "Assault is a serious charge. It will remain on your record until you are eighteen. I have read the extenuating circumstances concerning Mr. Robicheaux and his alleged participation in the death of two horses. However, Mr. Robicheaux's actions do not mitigate your crime. You are hereby ordered . . ."

This is where the judge tells me he's seen the tape, and I will never, ever go free.

". . . to have no contact with Mr. Hugh Robicheaux, and you will continue to be restricted from High Meadows Farm. Do I make myself clear?"

"Yes." Jas gasped in surprise.

"Speak up. I want to be sure you understand the importance of my order."

Jas bobbed her head. "Yes, Your Honor."

"Mr. Schuler, as the child's guardian, you are also responsible for making sure that your granddaughter has no contact with Mr. Robicheaux, his horses, or his property."

"I un-nerstand, Your Honor."

The judge swung his attention back to Jas, his gaze boring into hers. She began to tremble. *This is when he mentions the tape. This is where he arrests Chase.* "It is the order of the court that the terms of your probation and foster care be concluded." The gavel banged down. "Bailiff, clear the court for the next case."

Jas leaped in the air. She gratefully thanked

Mr. Petrie. Outside the courtroom, she hugged Grandfather and Miss Hahn, and thanked Miss Tomlinson and Mr. Eyler.

"Now let's go have that ankle bracelet removed," Miss Tomlinson said.

As Jas passed by Chase, he caught her hand. "See?" he whispered. "Everything turned out great. Hugh was bluffing."

She gave his hand a squeeze and then strode after Miss Tomlinson. Jas was glad Chase was feeling confident. But she knew better. For some reason, Hugh hadn't used the surveillance tape today. Even more puzzling, somehow he knew that she was searching for Whirlwind.

No, Hugh definitely wasn't bluffing, and he wasn't all talk.

Hugh had a spy.

Six

✤　✤　✤

THE ANKLE BRACELET PLOPPED TO THE FLOOR. Jas wiggled her leg. Without it, she felt a hundred pounds lighter. So did her spirits. She was no longer Jasmine Schuler, foster kid. And despite Hugh's threats, she felt freer than she had in months. So free, she skipped like a kid down the hall to join Miss Hahn and the others.

"You look as happy as Rose in the corn bin," Chase joked. Everybody laughed.

"And now for another treat," Miss Hahn said.

"Lunch? I'm starving," Chase said.

"Better than lunch." She exchanged a knowing look with Dr. Danvers.

Chase's jaw dropped. "You two are getting married while we're here at the courthouse?"

"Chase!" Jas poked him hard with her

elbow. Dr. Danvers guffawed, Grandfather chortled, and Miss Hahn turned bright red.

"Certainly not," she declared. "But Dr. Danvers did help me find a mobile home. We thought we'd go see it. If you two like it, we can move it to the farm on Monday."

"Yes! We'll like it, won't we?" Jas gave Grandfather a hug.

"Lunch first?" Chase pleaded.

They agreed to eat at a nearby diner. Jas linked her arm with her grandfather's. As she helped him through the courthouse door, she glanced behind her, expecting to see Hugh slouched in a dark corner, watching her with his predator eyes. The hearing was over, and the judge had ruled in Jas's favor. But that didn't mean she was free from Hugh Robicheaux. Her fight with him was just beginning.

"Incredible news," Jas told Shadow the next day as she snapped the cross ties to his halter. "My ankle transmitter is off. Now I can ride you any time I want."

Shadow pawed the aisle floor as if he didn't like what he heard. Laughing, Jas attacked his mud-caked coat with the curry. Last night it had finally rained after weeks of sun, and every horse had rolled.

Dirt flew as she rubbed, coating Jas's teeth. Still, she couldn't stop smiling. It was ten in the morning and too hot and buggy to ride. But after being on lockdown for so long, Jas wanted to prove that she could leave the property *any time she wanted.*

After Shadow was clean, she spritzed him with fly spray and tacked him up. When she checked the girth, he mouthed the bit and switched his tail. Jas rolled her eyes. The big guy was going to be a handful.

"Except I'm getting wise to your tricks," Jas said as she shoved her helmet on her head. She hunted for the mounting block, which had disappeared. Fortunately, she heard Chase outside.

She led Shadow from the barn. Chase was bent over, scrubbing buckets, singing a country song at the top of his lungs.

"I thought Rose was being murdered out here," Jas teased. "But it's only you butchering a song. Can you give me a leg up?"

"So you can have fun while *I* work?"

"Hey, this is my day to celebrate. I'll be back in time to do my share."

He straightened. His T-shirt was wet and molded to his slim torso. Hastily, Jas swung her eyes to Shadow. "Whoa, whoa," she said, even though he was standing still. Dropping the sponge in the bucket, Chase came up behind her. Reins gathered in her left hand, Jas held onto the pommel. She reached for the cantle of the saddle with her right hand. Chase cupped his hands under her bent left knee. "One, two, three!" On three, he tossed her into the saddle.

"Thanks." She smiled down at him as Shadow danced sideways. He didn't smile back. "What?"

He crossed his arms. "You didn't tell me everything Hugh said yesterday."

Blood rushed up her already hot neck. *How'd he know?* "Ummm." Bending, Jas checked her girth, then adjusted her stirrups. Shadow stomped impatiently. Finally she said, "You're right; there wasn't time. The bailiff had called my case."

"There's time now."

"I don't want to think about Hugh now. I'll tell you after my ride, okay?" Eager to get away from his accusing eyes, Jas squeezed her heels into Shadow's sides. He leaped forward, almost unseating her. She steered him through the open pasture gate, glancing behind her. She'd expected to see Chase still standing there, but he was gone.

She'd made a deal with him: no more secrets. So why hadn't she told him about Hugh's threats to the farm?

Shadow broke into a trot, his legs pounding with each long stride. She shook the question from her head. She needed to forget Hugh and concentrate on Shadow. The huge warm-blood was no push-button ride, and it took all Jas's balance and strength to keep her hands and seat steady.

"Easy, easy," she crooned as he headed toward the pond. She'd ridden him on the trail before, but never alone. She wasn't sure what to expect.

The hill was slippery from the rain, and she sat deep, trying to slow him. He fought her, shaking and rooting his head. He wanted to run, which would be disastrous. Shadow was hard enough to control in the ring. He'd be impossible in an open, muddy field. If he was to learn trail manners, she would have to be firm.

As they trotted across the pasture, Jas

looked up the brush-covered hill that sloped to the pond. The top was a perfect site for the mobile home they'd seen yesterday. It was rusted outside and musty inside, and Grandfather could barely make it up the makeshift steps. But it was free, a donation from a local farmer. Broken windows could be fixed. Moldy carpet could be replaced.

A duck took off from the pond with a whir of wings. Shadow exploded, throwing Jas onto his neck. She grabbed mane. Righting herself, she pulled his head around, doubling him into a circle. She'd ridden plenty of feisty horses before. But none as powerful as Shadow. *At least he's taking my mind off my troubles,* Jas thought as she gritted her teeth. But it also made her long for Whirlwind.

Jas had grown up with the mare. She'd been the first person to belly her, mount her, jump her, and show her, and she'd been her only groom. Whirlwind was graceful and sweet: Riding her had been a dream. They'd been in sync whether under saddle or over fences. Shadow was her challenge, Whirlwind her love. The pang grew sharper. Jas *had* to find her.

A snort startled her. Blowing wildly, Shadow

skittered from pretend demons in the underbrush. Jas legged him forward, and they followed the fence line to the log jump built into the board fence. "From my long-ago days of foxhunting," Miss Hahn had explained during the last trail ride. The logs were stacked three foot six; Shadow was such a talented jumper, he could take it at a trot.

She circled him, collecting him with rein, seat, and leg. When his one ear flicked and she knew he was listening, she pointed him toward the jump. He took off, sailed sky-high over the logs, and bounded wildly into the woods beyond. Jas ducked onto his neck to keep from getting knocked off by branches. Finally she got him back on the wide trail and trotting. Only then did she catch her breath.

"Don't you ever tire out?" she gasped. At last, he calmed to a jouncing walk. Flies buzzed around Jas's face, and sweat dripped from under her helmet. She swatted a deerfly on his neck, and he jumped sideways into a briar patch.

"*Walk!*" Jas growled. Miss Hahn had warned her that trail riding an ex–show jumper like Shadow took endless hours and bottomless patience.

Jas had both. Now that the stress of the court hearing was behind her and she wasn't on lockdown, she planned on working Shadow every day. She was going to step up her search for Whirlwind, too. Hugh's threats weren't going to stop her.

A fallen log crossed the trail ahead. Jas squeezed her legs against Shadow's sides, and he broke into a canter. Popping over it, they continued down the trail, his stride smooth and strong. "Atta boy," she praised.

Forty minutes and several miles later, they headed back up the hill through the pasture. Shadow's neck was dark with sweat, and the armpits of Jas's T-shirt were soaked. But the gelding walked calmly, and Jas let her reins dangle.

As they neared the farm, Jas spotted Mr. Muggins in the stable yard. He was scrubbing Rose's bristly back with a long-handled brush. In the riding ring, Rand was nailing a broken board. Chase waved at her from the quarantine paddock, where he was brushing out Wonder's tail. He'd been the one to volunteer to give the new rescue TLC. Already the colt's sores were healing, and he'd gained weight.

"Git! Git!" Jas heard Miss Hahn holler.

She stood in the doorway of the office trailer, shooing Heckle and Jeckle, the two burros, off the steps. Tilly, the border collie mix who followed Miss Hahn everywhere, barked at their heels. Devil the goat butted the bottom step, but the pesky burros were not budging until they got a treat.

When they reached the gate, Jas dismounted. She loosened the girth and led Shadow toward the office trailer after shutting the gate behind her. The burros had been rousted, and Miss Hahn sat on the steps, Tilly by her side. A phone book was in her lap, and a worried frown creased her brow.

"More bad news?" Jas asked, trying to sound upbeat.

"The hay supplier just called. He's out of hay. I've been calling around, but because of the drought, hay's in demand. Everyone wants too much money. And folks keep calling about horses they want us to take, because they have no grass and can't afford to feed them." Miss Hahn got slowly to her feet. "I can't tell them no. What's the point of a rescue farm if we can't rescue animals? So I'll just have to keep calling—someone's got to have hay." Sighing, she retreated into the office.

The door shut behind her, and Jas felt a

weight drop on her own shoulders. "Let's get you washed," she said, leading Shadow through the geese who were plucking weeds from around the trailer.

I can and I will destroy Miss Hahn and her precious farm. Over fifty animals had found a home at Second Chance Farm. Yet Hugh would have no qualms about ruining the refuge that Miss Hahn and the other volunteers had created for them.

Jas blinked back tears as she suddenly realized what she had to do. As much as she wanted to see Hugh prosecuted and as much as she loved Whirlwind, she couldn't put the farm and its animals in jeopardy.

She had to give up her fight against Hugh. She had to give up her search for Whirlwind.

Seven

⚜   ⚜   ⚜

HALTING SHADOW BEFORE THE STABLE DOOR-
way, Jas pressed her cheek against his sweaty
neck. "I don't want to lose you, either," she
whispered. "And who knows what Hugh will
do if I make him madder. He could burn down
the barn. Poison the—"

"Hey, Jas," Chase called from the fenced-in
area around the quarantine shed. "Hurry and
untack Shadow. I need help with Hope."

"I've gotta wash him first," she hollered
back, glad to be distracted from her gloomy
thoughts.

Mr. Muggins strode toward her, bucket
and brush in his hand. "I'll help," he said. Jas
stiffened. Since her day in court, she'd been
thinking about Hugh's spy. Was it someone at
the farm? Someone like Mr. Muggins, who was
a recent volunteer?

"I'm already soaked and I'm finished with Rose—or maybe I should say Rose is finished with me." Mr. Muggins tugged on his wet pant leg. "I'll get you fresh water and a sweat scraper."

"Thanks." Jas led Shadow down the aisle, where she put on his halter and untacked him. Back outside, she found a bucket of warm water and a scraper on the ground. Miss Hahn had introduced Mr. Muggins as a retired high school teacher with too much time on his hands. Or was that just a story he'd made up?

Jas would have to be careful about what she said around him.

"Fine-looking animal," Mr. Muggins told her when he came out of the barn and handed her a sponge.

"You should have seen him a month ago. Do you ride?"

He took the lead line from her. "My wife, Cindy, did. Before she died last year. Cancer."

"I'm sorry. My grandmother died from cancer, too." Jas slopped warm water on Shadow's back. Raising his head, the gelding wiggled his upper lip in delight. "I bet you miss her. It's been over a year, but I still miss my grandmother."

"Every day. I used to be Cindy's groom before she got sick, and we had to sell her mare. After she died, I realized how much I missed being around animals. A friend suggested volunteering here."

Using the scraper, Jas slicked off the excess water. Mr. Muggins's story sounded real, and since he knew what a sweat scraper was, he must have experience with horses like he said. Still, Jas wasn't taking any chances. "This place certainly needs volunteers," she said. "There's more work than workers, that's for sure. Thanks for your help."

She gave him a friendly smile, then walked Shadow into the ring to cool him off. Rand was banging nails into a post, replacing a broken board. Jas remembered the day Shadow jumped the five-foot fence into the neighboring field. It was the first time she suspected that the big horse they'd rescued was something special.

The ex–rodeo rider wore his signature sweat-stained cowboy hat and dusty jeans. "Need help, Rand? Mr. Muggins is looking for something to do."

He grunted. "The school teacher? No thanks. He already bent up a handful of nails." His gaze shifted to Shadow. "But if that bronco breaks down any of these new boards, you can pick up a hammer, young lady."

"That's fair."

He arced a squirt of tobacco juice over the fence. "Heard about yesterday. Glad to see that ankle bracelet's gone." Rand had begun volunteering soon after Jas had come to the farm, and he knew about her situation. Could *he* be the spy? she wondered. But she shook off the idea, realizing she was getting paranoid.

"I'm glad the annoying thing's gone, too," she said. Heckle and Jeckle trotted up, demanding pats. Jas scratched behind their fuzzy ears. As she led Shadow across the stable yard, Earl the rooster strutted in front as if leading a parade. When they entered the cool barn, the other horses whinnied greetings.

No matter how heavy her heart, Jas knew she had made the right decision. For the sake of the farm, she had to quit searching for Whirlwind.

Twining her fingers through Shadow's mane, she held tightly. The coarse hair bit into her skin. Hugh had told her that Whirlwind was safe and healthy. As much as she hated the idea of trusting him, on this, she had no choice.

"If Hope were a person, I'd say she was depressed." Chase knelt in the straw in the quarantine stall and snapped a leash to the pup's new collar. "She picks at her food, doesn't wag her tail, and ignores her rawhide chip."

Jas held out a bone-shaped cookie to the dog. Hope was curled in a ball, her eyes shut. "Come on, let's go for a walk," she coaxed. But the pup only tucked her nose deeper under her haunches.

"See what I mean? Every dog I know goes bonkers for walks," Chase said.

"I bet it was her mother's fault. She needs psychotherapy to uncover her hidden issues." Jas's joke sounded strained even to her.

"Thank you, Dr. Schuler, dog psychologist." When Jas didn't smile, he asked, "What are you so down about? Does it have something to do with what you won't tell me? Even though we had a deal?"

"You're right—I need to tell you." Jas took

a deep breath. "Hugh didn't just threaten me and you. He threatened Miss Hahn and the farm."

"What?" Chase jumped up so abruptly that Hope sprang nervously to her feet.

"His exact words were 'I can and I will destroy Diane and her precious farm.'"

"That jerk . . ."

"And I think he's got a spy who's reporting to him." Jas held the cookie inches from the pup's nose. Hope lifted her head and sniffed it. Taking the leash from Chase, she used the treat to lure the dog closer to the door. Then she fed half of it to her. Hope crunched slowly, without any joy.

"A spy?" Chase repeated, sounding unconvinced. "Isn't that a little James Bond?"

"How else would he know I'm looking for Whirlwind?" She gave him a sharp look, noticing the doubt in his expression. "You don't think Hugh's threats are serious, do you?"

"Well, yeah . . ." Chase had taken off his cap and was running his fingers through his sweaty hair.

"Hugh is serious. Look at it this way—any man who can murder two horses would have no problem burning down a barn full of them."

"You're right." Angrily, he slapped the cap back on his head.

"Don't say anything to Miss Hahn. She's got enough problems. We'll just have to be more careful about what we say." Jas picked up Hope. "Let's go for that walk." She carried the pup from the quarantine barn. Sam and Reese, the three-legged Lab, barked from the gate. "Look, there are some nice doggies who want to be friends." For a second, Hope's ears pricked. Then they flattened and she buried her nose in Jas's elbow.

"I definitely think there was another dog at Hope's old house," Jas said. "Maybe it died and that's why she's depressed." She looked over her shoulder at Chase. He was leaning against the doorjamb, frowning. His fingers were stuffed in his back pockets.

"We have to tell Miss Hahn," he said. "Especially if someone's skulking around, reporting to Hugh."

"No! She's already stressed over hay prices. Besides, it's not a problem anymore. I've decided to butt out and stop looking for Whirlwind. Let the insurance company's lawyers handle Hugh from now on."

"You? Butt out? Riiight."

"As long as Hugh's convicted of fraud, I'm okay. Hugh told me that Whirlwind is safe. I have to believe him. I'm sure he sold her for a lot of money. That means the person who bought her must value her."

Chase snorted. "Sure, as long as she can win trophies. Then what? A Mexican dog food factory?"

"Don't make it worse, Chase," Jas snapped. "It's not that I want to give up looking for her. I *have* to. I can't put the farm in jeopardy." She swung around, ending their conversation only to find Miss Hahn striding toward them.

"Jas, Chase, I'm glad you're both here," she called, wincing with each step as if her leg pained her more than usual. Her tan face was pale. Her lips were pinched angrily.

Jas clutched Hope, her heart thudding. *Please, not* more *bad news.*

Opening the gate, Miss Hahn slipped inside the quarantine enclosure without letting the other dogs through. "What's wrong?" Chase asked, hurrying over.

"Everything. I just got off the phone with

Jenkins. The insurance company is dropping its case against Hugh."

Jas's jaw dropped. "What? They can't do that!"

"Jenkins said they don't have enough proof to win a conviction." Miss Hahn's brown eyes glittered angrily. "The National Microchip Registry does not have Aladdin's microchip number on file. It's been too long since the horse supposedly died."

Jas moaned. She couldn't believe what she was hearing.

"And according to the insurance company," Miss Hahn continued, "the computer records and hard copies on Aladdin have been 'lost.'"

"You mean Hugh paid some office worker to destroy the information." Chase sent dirt clods into the air with a furious kick.

"Why didn't the insurance company or its lawyer have backups or duplicates or *something*?" Jas asked.

"They underestimated Hugh. Or, as Jenkins hinted, the lawyers knew from the beginning that they weren't going to prosecute him."

"I don't understand," Jas said, puzzled. "He committed a crime!"

"It's all about money," Miss Hahn explained. "Aladdin—Shadow—was insured for thirty grand. That's not a lot to an insurance company, especially when Hugh's lawyers have vowed to fight to the bitter end. The insurance company isn't interested in a lengthy and expensive case when the chances of winning are slim."

"So Hugh will get away with it—again." Jas felt sick. Turning, she dumped Hope in Chase's arms and started back toward the shed, too angry to talk.

"Jas," Miss Hahn said, stopping her. "I'm as disappointed as you. I was hoping that we could finally expose Hugh, too. And I know your heart is set on finding Whirlwind. There was a chance that information on her whereabouts might have surfaced during the trial."

Jas shrugged, pretending she didn't care, but her eyes were blurry with tears.

"I know Dr. Danvers wasn't very encouraging," Miss Hahn continued. "But there must be some way we can find her."

"No. There isn't," Jas said tonelessly.

"You haven't given up, have you?"

"Tell her," Chase said to Jas.

"Tell me what?" Miss Hahn looked back and forth between the two.

"If you don't tell her, I will."

Jas glared at Chase, her arms folded. He glared back, just as determined. "Okay." She took a deep breath. "Hugh was at the courthouse yesterday. He threatened you and the farm if I didn't back off."

"His exact words were 'I can and *I will* destroy Diane and her precious farm,'" Chase said.

Miss Hahn jerked as if she'd been slapped. "That arrogant—! Jas, I don't care what Hugh threatened. We are not giving up. We're going to find Whirlwind, and we're going to convince that chicken-liver Jenkins and his lawyers that they need to prosecute Hugh. If they won't, I'll get Officer Lacey and the county to charge Hugh with cruelty to animals. He killed two horses for no reason, and if word gets out, there are enough animal lovers in this area to tar and feather him."

As Jas listened to Miss Hahn rant, she felt a tendril of hope. Still, she was afraid to even think that maybe they could get Hugh.

Miss Hahn patted her leg. "You know, if I'd dealt with Hugh Robicheaux twenty years ago, he wouldn't be so cocky today. During a show, he caused me to have an accident. I thought we were friends, but to him, friend-ship was nothing compared to winning."

"What did he do?" Jas asked.

"He loosened my girth before a jumping class. The saddle slipped and I crashed into a fence. Broke my leg in four places. Hugh won the class, of course. I had no proof or I would have confronted him then. So if he wants to take me on now, I'm ready."

"Are you sure?" Jas asked. "This could get ugly."

"Not as ugly as a bunch of ticked-off horse lovers," Miss Hahn declared.

Chase grinned at Jas. "See? I told you that you needed to tell her."

A tiny smile lifted Jas's lips. "You were right."

"As always." Chase shifted Hope in his arms.

"Still, there's the problem of finding Whirl-wind," Jas said. "I sure don't have any brilliant ideas."

Miss Hahn's eyes brightened. "It just so happens that Dr. Danvers is coming over tonight for fried chicken. He's bringing your grandfather. So if we put our five heads together . . ."

Jas reached for Hope. "Four heads," she corrected. She glanced teasingly up at Chase as she took the dog from his arms.

"Four?" Miss Hahn crooked her brow.

Jas burst out laughing, suddenly feeling hopeful and downright giddy about finding Whirlwind. "If we're trying to come up with brilliant ideas, then Chase's head doesn't count!"

Eight

❧   ❧   ❧

"HUGH ISN'T THE FIRST TO KILL A HORSE FOR money," Miss Hahn said. She passed the platter of fried chicken to Jas, who sat next to her at the kitchen table. Grandfather was on Jas's other side so she could cut his food. Across the table, Chase and Dr. Danvers attacked their food as if starving. "One of the worst cases of fraud happened in the early 1990s."

Jas placed a thigh on her plate. It was already filled with potato salad and green beans from the garden. "What happened?"

"Some of the top riders and wealthiest owners in the business paid a lowlife named Tommy Burns to kill their horses."

Chase nodded as he shoveled a forkful of beans in his mouth. "I memember."

"How could you *memember*?" Jas asked. "You weren't even born."

"Read about it."

Jas feigned shock. "You read?"

He tossed a slice of carrot from the salad at her. "Hey!" She picked up a chunk of celery, ready to retaliate. Sam, who had been sleeping quietly on the floor, perked up.

"Manners, *children*," Miss Hahn warned.

"I read about it, too," Dr. Danvers said. "The case was tried in Chicago in a federal court."

"Will someone tell me what happened?" Jas repeated.

"Will someone pass me the 'icken." Grandfather looked pointedly at her.

"Sorry." She put a drumstick on his plate.

"In a nutshell, nineteen people were indicted for killing at least thirteen horses for insurance money," Miss Hahn explained.

"How'd they kill them?" Jas asked.

"Electrocution mostly," Dr. Danvers said. "In one case, a horse named Empire was galloped until sweaty. Then he was put in a clean stall and electrocuted. Based on the sweat and clean stall, the vet ruled colic."

Jas set down her fork, suddenly not smiling. She thought of the dead horse in Whirlwind's paddock.

"What I don't understand is why they

would risk their reputations for money," Chase said, adding, "This chicken is delicious, Miss Hahn."

Grandfather waved his drumstick. "Greed."

"You're right," Miss Hahn said. "They needed cash, they had an insured horse that wasn't performing, and they knew a guy who could kill it, no problem. And they were pompous enough to think they'd never get caught."

"Like Hugh," Chase said.

Miss Hahn set the salad bowl next to Jas. "All the people charged were prominent in the horse world. George Lindemann Jr. was a former member of the United States Equestrian Team. Barney Ward was a grand prix rider. At the time, those of us who loved horses couldn't believe they'd actually done it. Jas, more salad?"

"No thank you," Jas whispered. She'd lived at High Meadows Farm for five years. Not once had she suspected that Hugh was capable of murder. "How did I not know?" Raising her eyes, she looked around the table. "How did I miss the signs?"

"What signs?" Chase asked.

"That Hugh could kill a horse. They were right in front of me. One, he bought and sold horses only for profit." She counted off on her fingers. "Two, I never saw him actually pat a horse. Three, a horse to him wasn't a living, breathing animal, it was a dollar sign." She laid her hand on Grandfather's arm. "Remember Little Bit? The two-year-old with the bad feet? Hugh sold him for some ridiculous amount to a family with more money than sense. The daughter was going to train him to be a jumper. Later you told me that the family put the colt down because he was constantly lame. If Hugh had sold him for a pleasure horse"—her voice grew angrier—"that never would have happened!"

"Jas, I vetted the horse for the family," Dr. Danvers pointed out. "I told them he wouldn't stay sound for jumping."

"But Hugh convinced them otherwise," she said. "I was there. I should have said something." Pushing back her chair, she jumped up. Sam scrambled to his feet with a startled *woof*. "I could have saved Little Bit. I should have saved Whirlwind!"

Chase stood up just as quickly. A string

bean clung to the front of his T-shirt. "You make it sound like it was your fault, not Hugh's."

"It was. I should have known what he was going to do. I should have stopped him." Tossing down her napkin, she spun to leave the table. Grandfather grabbed her wrist, and she felt his old strength in the grasp of his fingers. "No, Jas, you 'ere just a kid."

"Your grandfather's right," Dr. Danvers said. "If we had known, we would have stopped him. We were adults, yet we didn't see the signs, either."

Miss Hahn gave Chase a firm look and then pointed to Jas's plate. "Sit down. Both of you. If we're going to find Whirlwind, we need to be thinking clearly. Not emotionally. Okay?"

Jas sat with an unladylike thump. Beside her, Sam slid again to the floor.

"Well, I'd be emotional, too," Chase said.

She shot him a grateful look for sticking up for her. Picking up her fork, she speared a lettuce leaf. "So, does anyone have an idea how we can find Whirlwind?" She tried to keep her voice from shaking.

"I do." Miss Hahn dabbed her mouth with a napkin. "I'm thinking that Hugh used an agent to sell her. He would not have contacted buyers directly. Too risky."

Jas's eyes widened. "You're right. And if we can find the agent, we can find who he sold Whirlwind to."

"Unless the agent is in on the scam, too," Dr. Danvers cautioned.

"My guess is the agent would *not* be in on the scam," Miss Hahn said. "I think that's one reason Hugh got away with the bogus sale the first time with Aladdin/Shadow. He didn't want anyone else involved who could implicate him."

"So the agent believed it was a legitimate sale." Jas turned toward Grandfather. "Who would Hugh have used?"

Reaching behind her, Miss Hahn pulled out a kitchen drawer. "Let me get a pencil and paper. We'll make a list."

"Anthony Bixby." Dr. Danvers waved his fork in the air. "He's in Middleburg and was often at the farm."

"'enny Ferraro," Grandfather chimed in.

"Enny?" Miss Hahn repeated. "Spell that for me."

"He means Jenny," Jas said.

"And Scott Black," Miss Hahn added as

she wrote. "He's from Lexington and a big name in the hunter-jumper circuit. He's been around as long as I have." While they finished eating, several more names were suggested.

"Let's start calling them right now," Jas said excitedly.

"No," Miss Hahn said. "This list is going to Mister Jenkins."

"I thought you said the insurance company was dropping the case," Chase said.

"They were." Miss Hahn faced Jas. "But tomorrow, you and I are paying Mr. Jenkins a visit. We'll show him there's enough evidence to convict Hugh. We'll convince him not to drop the case."

Jas nodded eagerly. "Yes! Let's do it."

Later, when the others were gone, Miss Hahn washed dishes while Jas wiped off the kitchen table. "Eww. Chase is a pig," Jas said. "There's food everywhere. He should eat with Rose."

"He is messy." Miss Hahn set the last glass in the drainer. She looked thoughtfully at Jas and then said, "You know, Jas, you don't have to keep running away."

Jas deliberately sponged up the last of the crumbs before asking, "What do you mean?"

"Every time we discuss something tough, you want to run from it—and us. Like tonight."

Jas gave her a funny look. "I wasn't running away. I was frustrated and upset."

"I know. But if your grandfather hadn't stopped you, you would have left the table in a huff. Believe it or not, we share your feelings. If we stick together, we can accomplish something. Like the list we made. That's a solid start to getting Hugh."

Jas blinked at her.

"Anyway, I know these past months have been hard. I'm not trying to be critical, but think about it." Draping the dishtowel over the side of the sink, Miss Hahn turned to put away the dried plates.

Jas plopped the dirty sponge in the sink. Miss Hahn was right. Ever since the day she'd attacked Hugh with the hoof pick, she had been afraid to trust anyone. When she first came to Second Chance Farm, she'd even accused her former foster mother of being in cahoots with Hugh. She thought she'd gotten better about the trust thing. But hadn't she just this afternoon tried to keep Hugh's threats a secret? Only Chase's pigheaded persistence had made her tell Miss Hahn.

That meant she hadn't gotten any better. And if she really wanted to find Whirlwind, she would have to let down her guard. Like Miss Hahn said, she'd have to stop running away.

Nine

❧   ❧   ❧

"I DON'T KNOW, CHASE," JAS SAID AS SHE FOL-
lowed him and Wonder into the quarantine paddock the next morning. After six days of being
at the farm, the colt's stride was stronger and his
sores were healing. On the other side of the paddock, Rand was banging a nail into a board.

"Don't know what?" Chase asked, raising
his voice so he could be heard over the hammering.

"I don't know if we can convince Mr. Jenkins." Jas carried an old towel in one hand, a
brush tucked under her arm. "Easy." When
Chase halted Wonder, she gently rubbed the
colt from his withers to his rump, getting him
used to being touched all over.

"Maybe you can't convince him." Chase
wore baggy cutoffs, and his cap was on backward, looking cute in a grungy sort of way.

"Never say *can't*. See? He's standing quietly." She pointed to Wonder, trying to keep her attention on the horse, not Chase. "I bet I can convince him to stand still if I flap the towel around his legs."

"No, doofy, I mean Mr. Jenkins."

"Oh." Jas laughed. Twirling the towel into a rolled strip, she snapped the end at Chase's bare calf. Wonder skittered sideways.

"Hey, what was that for?"

"*That* was for calling me doofy. And for doubting my powers of persuasion." She patted Wonder. "Don't worry, that wasn't aimed at *you*."

"You were the one who said you couldn't convince Mr. Jenkins."

"I'm just afraid we don't have enough real evidence to change his mind." Jas ran the towel down the colt's face. "Hugh knows how to cover his tracks. What if we can't find the agent who sold Whirlwind?"

"We're in trouble. And even if we do find the agent, he could be in on the scam. I bet Hugh has partners in crime all over the place."

"I agree. I know for sure that Jenny Ferraro is a shark. I'd ride Hugh's horses when she'd bring clients to the farm. Not only did she order me around, but she was also a barracuda when it came to closing a deal. One day, she was showing a client one of Hugh's jumpers who had a nasty scar on his leg. She came early. In the trunk of her car, she had a bag filled with cans of shoe polish. She found the right color to match the horse. When she was done rubbing polish on that horse's leg, the scar had disappeared."

Chase scratched Wonder's neck. "This guy would need a whole can to cover his scars."

"He's too knock-kneed to be a show horse, anyway." Jas pointed to the colt's front legs. "You know, I loved showing. But never once did I wonder if the horse loved it, too."

"I bet some like it," Chase said. Jas gave him such a shocked look that he held up his hand in defense. "A few who love trotting around a dusty ring in the broiling heat."

"You are so busted." Jas laughed. "I knew you secretly wanted to wear breeches and black boots."

Chase rolled his eyes. "Give me a break."

"I bet Shadow would love showing again."

"He'd probably eat the competition."

"He's not *that* ferocious." Jas snapped him again on the leg.

"What was *that* for?" He grabbed the end of the towel and yanked. She flew toward him, falling against his chest.

"Whoa," he said, more to her than to Wonder, who jerked backward. Pulling away, the colt trotted across the paddock. Chase, however, didn't let Jas go. One arm lightly circled her waist. Jas's cheeks flamed and her heart pounded at his closeness. She pressed her palms against his sweaty shirt, afraid to tip up her chin for fear he would kiss her.

Or was she afraid he *wouldn't* kiss her?

"What are you two greenhorns doing?" Rand strode toward them, holding Wonder's rope. Jas and Chase sprang apart. "Trying to teach the new rescue to be a runaway?"

"Uh, no," Chase stammered. "We were just . . . um . . . getting him used to . . . um."

"Mushy romance?" Rand guffawed. Jas picked up the towel and brush, her whole face burning.

Rand tossed the rope to Chase. "Don't worry. I was young once." He winked, and Chase grinned sheepishly.

Embarrassed, Jas tackled the colt's mane with the brush. *Thank you, Rand, for interrupting.* She didn't want to ruin the friendship she had with Chase. They'd kissed once before, but it had been so brief she was sure he at least had forgotten it. A second kiss might mean they were more than friends. And that would change everything.

Fists propped on his hips, Rand appraised the colt. His one cheek bulged with tobacco. "What a sorry-looking critter," he finally said. "Here I'm volunteering at the farm to pay penance for the bucking horses I spurred. But in all my rodeo days, I never intentionally abused a horse."

"Obviously the meth dealer's first priority wasn't his pets," Chase said.

Jas nodded in agreement, her attention riveted on a burr in the colt's mane. Her pulse had slowed. Her brain was returning to normal. *Not that I am ever normal around Chase.* Which had to stop if she was going to find Whirlwind.

"No excuse." Rand spit tobacco juice to the side. "The druggy's wife could have called and told us to pick the horse up before it starved. Second Chance Farm is practically right next door to them. We would have gladly hauled the colt out of there."

Hauled the colt out of there. Jas inhaled sharply as the words hit her. "That's it!" She spun to face them.

"What's it?" Chase asked.

"That's how we can find Whirlwind!"

Chase and Rand gave her blank stares. Wonder lowered his head to grab a bite of grass.

"Someone had to haul her from High Meadows that day," she explained excitedly. "If we find that person, we can find Whirlwind."

"Couldn't Hugh have hauled her?" Chase asked.

"No. Phil Sparks and Grandfather had the stock trailer. Hugh wasn't licensed to drive the big van."

Taking off his cowboy hat, Rand scratched his head. "You lost me."

Jas froze, suddenly realizing how much she'd just blurted to Rand. He knew about her arrest and about the insurance scam. Neither were a secret. But secrets *were* leaking to Hugh.

You've got to stop searching for Whirlwind, Hugh had threatened. What if it *was* Rand tipping him off?

Jas eyed the grizzled cowboy. There were at least a dozen volunteers. Should she be suspicious of all of them? Or should she follow Miss Hahn's advice: *If we stick together, we can accomplish something.* Rand had worked around horses all his life. What if he knew something that could help? And hadn't Jas decided just last night that she needed to be more trusting?

Rand whacked the dust off his cowboy hat, waiting for a reply. She cut her eyes to Chase. He was bent over, picking out Wonder's front hoof, no help at all.

Taking a deep breath, Jas decided to trust him. She hoped she wouldn't regret it.

"Last night we made a list." Jas told Rand about the half-dozen agents who might have worked for Hugh. "Miss Hahn and I are seeing Mr. Jenkins this afternoon. We're going to convince him that we can find Whirlwind. One way is through the agent who might have sold her. Another is finding the person who hauled her from the farm. Does that make sense?"

He nodded. "Yup."

"Makes sense to me, too." Chase set down Wonder's hoof and straightened. "I say we go through the Yellow Pages and start calling, right now."

"Nope." Rand settled his cowboy hat back on. "Person you're looking for ain't going to be listed in the Yellow Pages."

"What do you mean?" Jas asked.

"A reputable hauler has to keep tidy records for taxes and insurance. This Robicheaux guy doesn't want a record of where his mare went."

"Good point. How do we find him, then?" Jas asked.

"Ask around. I know a few guys who haul horses as a side job. And I bet your grandfather knows some, too."

Jas smiled. She'd been right to trust him. "Thanks."

"Anything to help a lady." He touched his hat brim before striding back to his fence-patching job.

"A *lady*?" Chase snorted. "That old man needs glasses."

"Oh, shut up." Jas elbowed him in the ribs.

"You know . . ." Crossing his arms, Chase

studied Rand, who was pulling his hammer from his tool belt.

"You know . . . what?" Jas asked, panicking. Did Chase think Rand might be the spy, too?

"My idea is better," he finished his thought. "About the Yellow Pages."

"Oh." Jas blew out a relieved breath. "I thought you were going to say Rand was the person reporting to Hugh. Now I realize you're just jealous of him."

Chase gave an exaggerated shrug. "Nah." Turning, he bent to pick up Wonder's left hind foot. The colt swished his tail in annoyance. "Rand's no spy."

Jas glanced over at the cowboy, who was nailing boards again. "How do you know? He showed up at the farm about the same time I did. Doesn't that seem a strange coincidence?"

"Volunteers are in and out of this place all the time. Besides, he doesn't sneak around listening at doors and sending messages in code."

"Would you be serious? He could have bugged the office or something."

Setting down Wonder's foot, Chase rose up. "Okay, I'll keep my eye on him—just for you," he said before crossing behind the colt and picking up his right foot.

"Good idea. Speaking of ideas, did you ever ask your dad if he had any suggestions about finding Whirlwind?"

"All he said was that most insurance companies have investigators they can hire who specialize in fraud."

"I'll mention it to Mr. Jenkins. Thanks— for everything."

"No need to thank me." He stared sideways at her, Wonder's leg secure against his bent knee. "It's my job." Pointing the dirty hoof pick at her, he drawled, "Because I'm Bond. James Bond."

Jas laughed. "You have seen *Goldfinger* way too many times."

Sam followed Jas down the rocky driveway. Hope, who was finally out of quarantine, trotted by her side on a leash. The mobile home was being delivered this morning, and Jas was checking to see if the truck had arrived.

She stopped at the sign by the entrance: S COND CHANCE ARM. No one had gotten around to fixing it. Jas ran her fingers over the bumpy black wood letters, remembering the day the social worker had driven her to the farm. She'd compared everything—fencing, barns, horses, and pastures—to High Meadows and found it sadly lacking. Now she was happy to call the tumbledown place home.

And she wasn't going to let Hugh ruin it.

Yesterday, Jas and Miss Hahn had met with Mr. Jenkins. Not only had he agreed to pursue charges against Hugh, but he was also assigning an investigator to the case. He handed Jas a card that said M. BAYLOR. "Best in the business," Mr. Jenkins had assured them.

A truck rumbling up the road interrupted Jas's thoughts. She waved at the driver to stop. "Turn left at the open gate," she instructed. "Follow the lane to the top of the hill. We'll be waiting."

Jas hurried back up the driveway. Miss Hahn and Grandfather were sitting on the front porch swing. "It's here!" she called as she ran past them to the side yard. A path led into the field. The trail branched—left to the pond, right up the hill.

When she reached the top, the truck was

winding toward her from the main road. Several days ago, one of the farm's donors had bulldozed a flat spot. Then electric lines had been run, a well dug, and septic tank installed. Yesterday, Jas had used the string trimmer and Chase had used the Bush Hog to cut the unruly grass and weeds.

A dog bayed, and Tilly and Reese bounded through the brush. They greeted Jas with eager licks, as if they hadn't seen her in days. Hope pricked her ears. But then she plopped to the ground and placed her chin on her paws.

The little dog was eating better but still seemed sad. Officer Lacey had set a Havahart trap at the meth dealer's place. He'd baited it with hamburger, hoping to entice Hope's friend—if there was one. So far, all he'd trapped was a possum.

Jas heard wheezing and panting. Sam was hobbling up the hill, his tail wagging with each step. Grandfather and Miss Hahn straggled behind him.

"You made it." Jas trotted down the slope to meet them. Linking her arm through her grandfather's, she pulled him the rest of the way.

While he caught his breath, they watched the driver haul the mobile home to the top of the hill. "Where ya want it?" the man shouted.

"Right there." Jas pointed. Their new home would overlook the barns, pastures, and pond. On the right, a grove of locust trees would shade the kitchen. In back, there was enough sun for next year's vegetable garden.

"What a gorgeous view," Miss Hahn said. In the distance, they could see the wavy blue line of the Allegheny Mountains.

Jas squeezed her grandfather's arm. "What do you think, Grandfather?"

"It's perfect," he said, tears shimmering in his eyes.

"Yes," Jas whispered. "It is."

The driver shifted gears, and the mobile home jerked forward. One tire bumped over a protruding rock, and a piece of window glass shattered and crashed to the ground.

The driver flashed a toothy grin out the open window. "Needs a little TLC," he hollered.

"Sir, watch out for the—" Jas shouted.

Too late, the front tire lurched into a rain-washed rut they'd trimmed around. Swearing loudly, the driver braked. The truck jerked to a halt, and the trailer door crashed open. With a screech of metal, it tore off the top hinge.

Okay, our new home isn't exactly perfect. Jas sighed as the door flapped like a lopsided mouth. *But it's good enough.*

Ten

❖ ❖ ❖

"I KNOW—THE PLACE STINKS LIKE MOUSE poop," Jas admitted to Chase. He stood in the living room of the mobile home, holding his nose. "But be a man and toughen up."

Jas was on her knees, tearing out chunks of rain-soaked carpet. For two days she'd scrubbed counters and walls, while Miss Hahn and Mr. Muggins had dragged out trash bags bulging with empty food cans and fast-food wrappers.

"Mouse poop I can handle," Chase said. "It's the other smell. Like something's dead."

"Gross." Lucy's voice came from behind Chase. Jas tensed. She hadn't realized the older girl had arrived with Chase. "What is that smell?"

Rrrrip. Jas tore out another soggy section of carpet. What was Lucy doing with Chase?

He said he'd been gone for two days visiting relatives with his family. Or had he really been off with Lucy?

Oh, stop, Jas scolded herself. *That is a stupid thought.* Sitting on her heels, she blew through clenched teeth, furious for feeling jealous. Chase wasn't her boyfriend. *And why do I care that Lucy thinks this place smells gross?*

Walking over, Chase stared down at Jas.

"How was your trip?" she asked. Leaning forward, she started on another stubborn strip.

"Fun. Miniature golf and old home movies. You know, grandparent stuff."

No, I don't know grandparent stuff, Jas realized. Her grandparents had been a mom and a dad to her.

"I bet you were a cutie-pie in those old movies, Chase," Lucy cooed as she walked around the living room. Jas half expected her to whip out a clipboard and inspection sheet. Buckled paneling—check. Rain-stained ceiling—check.

Chase squatted next to Jas. "How about if I get a chain saw? I love hacking up things. Maybe there's a dead body buried beneath the flooring."

"Thanks, but I can handle the dirty work." Jas wiped the sweat off her brow. It was hot outside and stifling inside. "Rand needs help building the new steps. He's making a railing for Grandfather."

Chase stood up. "We saw him when we came in. I'll give him a hand." When Chase left, Jas glanced over her shoulder. Lucy was peeking cautiously into the kitchen. She wore a turquoise tank top, white short shorts, and jeweled flip-flops. Her legs were smooth and tan and didn't have a single bruise, scrape, or scab. In her arms, she held a box with a picture of a microwave on the side.

"Whatcha got, Luce?" Jas forced herself to be friendly.

"A housewarming present from my mom."

"Thanks. We'll need it. I'm not sure the oven works."

Setting the box on the kitchen counter, Lucy looked into the sink and grimaced. "Eww."

Jas tossed a strip of carpet into the trash can. "Quit frowning, Luce, or you'll need Botox."

"Not likely," Lucy retorted, but she immediately smoothed her forehead with two fingers.

"How will you stand living here without air-conditioning?" she asked, fanning herself.

"We'll do fine." Jas's voice tightened. Then she reminded herself that the older girl wasn't being mean. She was just being Lucy. "Make sure you thank your mom for the microwave."

"Yeah, well . . ." Without offering to help, she sauntered to the doorway and jumped to the ground outside. A second later, Jas heard her talking to Chase and Rand. She pictured the scene. Lucy would have one hand propped on her hip. The other would be flipping her bangs off her forehead while she chatted up the two guys. Rand's eyes would be hound-dog eager. Chase would be drooling.

Jas rubbed her lower back. Her jeans were covered with rotted carpet fibers. The skin on her arms and hands was gray with dust. She couldn't blame Lucy for not wanting to help. And her own frustration had nothing to do with Lucy's flirtations. It had been two days, and still there was no word from M. Baylor. Jas was losing patience.

Grabbing the utility scissors, she attacked another section of carpet. She sawed and snipped until her hand ached.

"Where do you want these?" Chase hollered about twenty minutes later.

"These what?" She looked over her shoulder.

Chase slid two boxes through the doorway. "Dishes."

"Dishes?" Jas stood, groaning at the pain in her knees. Chase took a running start and leaped into the living room, landing beside her. "Who brought them?" she asked.

"Mrs. Quincey."

"Oh, her." Jas knew her as "the old lady who volunteered in the office Monday mornings." Bending, she poked through the silverware, dishes, glasses, hot mitts, and cooking utensils. "That was really nice."

"She's moving into assisted living and needs to get rid of her kitchen stuff."

"That's *really* nice." Jas held up a blue-rimmed plate. "At High Meadows Farm, no one was nice."

Pulling out a hand beater, Chase whirled it next to her ear. "No one?"

"Grandfather, of course, and Grandmother when she was alive." Carefully, Jas unwrapped two flower-painted glasses and set them on a cupboard shelf. "And Phil Sparks, I guess.

When my grandmother died, Hugh got meaner. Maybe when she was alive, she'd forced him to be human."

"So even *you* were meaner then?" Chase handed her a plate.

She ignored his teasing. "Not mean. Just *not nice*. Now that I look back, I see that living there was changing me."

"You were turning into a mini Hugh!" Chase gasped with horror.

"Are you ever serious?" Jas poked him with a spatula, then placed it in a drawer. "I'm trying to say something profound here."

"Mini Hugh wasn't profound?"

"Actually it was. Maybe Whirlwind 'dying' was the best thing that ever happened to me. It got me away from there."

"Plus it got you sent to Second Chance Farm. Where I met you," Chase said. His back was to her as he reached up to put a plate on the shelf, so she couldn't see his face. But she could tell by his voice that for once he wasn't joking.

"That too," she said, realizing how fast her heart was suddenly beating. Quickly, she banged shut the drawer. "I'll put the rest away later. I've had enough for one day."

Turning away, she washed her hands under the kitchen faucet, which spat rust-colored water, and dried them on a paper towel. "Is Rand finished working? I don't hear any hammering."

"He and Lucy went to feed. It's almost four."

"So you're free to do some detective work?"

Facing her, he gave her his usual teasing grin. "There really *was* a body under the floorboards?"

"No, doofy." Jas tossed the wadded up towel at him. "I'm tired of waiting for Investigator Baylor to show up. Grandfather and Rand gave me some names of people who haul horses in the area." She pulled a scrap of paper from her back pocket. "I say we find the Yellow Pages and start phoning."

Chase pointed a wooden spoon at her. "I knew it was a good idea."

Fifteen minutes later, they sat side by side on the porch swing. Jas sipped lemonade while Chase drank a soda. His left leg was next to her right one. Sawdust clung to the golden hairs on his knees. Her jeans were sprinkled with dirt. Both of them were thirsty, hot, and smelled like sweat.

Jas smiled, liking the closeness. "Horse

haulers. Horse transport," she guessed as she flicked through the Yellow Pages. "I'm not even sure what to look under."

"Horse killers?" Chase suggested. "Oh, wait, that would be under *R*, for Robicheaux."

"Wait. Here it is. Equine Transport Services. Only two companies listed." She punched a set of numbers into the portable phone. Taking it from her, Chase pressed the OFF button. "Why'd you do that?" she asked.

"Do you know what you're going to say? We don't want to make them suspicious."

"Oh, right." She gnawed her bottom lip, thinking.

"Does Hugh have a secretary or accountant? You could pretend to be one of them, checking on a bill or something."

"Good idea." She flipped the pages until she came to Accountants. She randomly selected the name of an accountant to use, then dialed one of the horse transporters.

"Hello. My name is Esther uh . . . Smith . . . of EZ Bookkeeping and Accounting in Harrisonburg. I work for Mr. Hugh Robicheaux at High Meadows Farm in Stanford." As Jas spun her story, Chase gave her a thumbs-up. "You sent an invoice dated June first for hauling a horse from his farm. I need to verify that information. Thank you. I'll hold." She covered the mouthpiece. "They're checking."

Minutes later, the woman on the other end said, "I'm sorry, Ms. Smith. There is no record of our company hauling a horse for Mr. Robicheaux."

Jas thanked her. "Let's try the second number." Chase took the phone from her. "This time, I want to talk."

"Okay, but do *not* tell them your real name."

Chase gave her an "I'm not that stupid" look and then said, "Hello, is this Highsmith Transport? My name is Jim Bond from EZ Bookkeeping. . . ."

Jas rolled her eyes.

"Nope," Chase said minutes later. "Highsmith has never heard of the notorious Hugh. Let's try the list your grandfather came up with."

"I've already found the phone number for the first name: Tommy Looney."

"Looney? As in crazy? That sounds sketchy."

Jas took the phone from him. "My turn."

This time when she dialed, instead of a crisp-talking receptionist, a guy answered with a sleepy "yup."

"Is this Mr. Looney?" Jas asked.

"Who wants to know?"

"This is Esther Smith of EZ Bookkeeping and Accounting in Harrisonburg. I work for Mr. Hugh Robicheaux at High Meadows Farm in Stanford." She launched into her spiel.

When she finished, there was a long pause punctuated by several coughs. "June first you say?" Looney finally asked.

The way he emphasized the date made Jas catch her breath. "Yes. I have the invoice right in front of me."

"Invoice? Lady, you've definitely got the wrong guy."

"Are you sure Mr. Looney? Your name—"

"I'm *sure*." His tone was gruff. "I ain't never hauled no chestnut horse from the Robicheaux place." The phone clicked off.

The hairs rose on the back of Jas's neck. Wide-eyed, she turned toward Chase. "We found him," she whispered, her voice trembling. "Hugh hired Tommy Looney to haul Whirlwind."

"How do you know?"

"He said he doesn't remember hauling a chestnut horse from the Robicheaux place."

"That's it?"

"That's enough, Chase," Jas exclaimed. "Don't you see? I never told him the horse was chestnut!"

Eleven

❦   ❦   ❦

CHASE'S JAW DROPPED. "THAT'S DARN FINE detective work, Ms. Smith."

"Thank you, Mr. Bond." Jas chewed a ragged nail. "Only, now what? He denied it and hung up on me. So it's not like he's going to tell me where he took Whirlwind. And it's not like the police can bust in and arrest him."

"M. Baylor can," Chase said. "Not arrest him but find out where Looney took Whirlwind."

Jas gave him a doubtful look.

"PIs can do anything," he insisted. "Haven't you watched detective shows on television?"

She shook her head. "I need to talk to Grandfather. He knows Tommy Looney. I bet he could find out where he took Whirlwind. I'll call him."

"Isn't he moving here tomorrow?"

"I can't wait until then." Bolting off the swing, Jas began to pace along the porch, the phone clutched in her hand. Hastily, she punched in the numbers for her grandfather, but he was in physical therapy. "I'll call Mr. Jenkins." But the insurance agency was closed. "It must be after five." Frustrated, she tossed the phone at Chase, who caught it with one hand.

"Where's Miss Hahn?" Chase asked. "We can tell her."

"Off with Mr. Muggins, picking up hay. We're supposed to help them unload it."

Chase finished his soda. "When she gets here, we'll tell her what we found out."

"Not in front of Mr. Muggins," Jas said quickly.

Chase arched one brow. "Right . . . that spy thing." He crushed the empty soda can. "Let's call your grandfather later. Then tomorrow we'll call Mr. Jenkins and find out where this Baylor person is." When Jas strode in front of Chase, he caught her wrist. "Does that sound like a plan?"

She nodded impatiently. "It's just that this is the first real break, and I'm tired of waiting. I want to find Whirlwind. *Now.*"

"We will." Chase pulled her down beside him on the swing, and his skin was warm against hers. "I promise."

The next day, Jas stood in the middle of the mobile home's living room. That morning, she'd finished tearing up the carpet. She'd scrubbed the walls, ceiling, and floor. After everything had dried, she'd vacuumed with Miss Hahn's Shop-Vac. The place was clean but depressing. There were no curtains, no frills, and—except for two beds—no furniture.

They'd lived in a mobile home at High Meadows Farm, so it wasn't as if Jas expected luxury. But it had been bright and homey with Grandmother's plump pillows, framed photos, and hooked rugs. Jas had no doubt that by now Hugh had destroyed her family's every possession and keepsake. They were starting over.

She ran her fingers through her hair. It was tangled with soap scum and dust. They'd never been able to contact Grandfather yesterday, and now he was due any minute. She couldn't bear to think of him coming into *this*.

Going outside, she placed two pots of geraniums on either side of the new stairs that

Rand and Chase had built. At least he would be greeted with a sturdy railing and bright flowers. Weary, she plopped on the bottom step and glanced down the hill. The underfoot gang hung outside the office trailer, which meant Miss Hahn was inside. When Chase and Jas had told her about Tommy Looney, she'd gotten excited. She had promised to call Mr. Jenkins this morning to tell him and to ask when M. Baylor was coming.

Now it was early afternoon. Jas jiggled her leg, anxious to find out what Miss Hahn had discovered. But she had one more task to finish before Grandfather's arrival.

She headed back into the mobile home, which had two tiny bedrooms. Social services had given them money for mattresses. She and Miss Hahn had found two single bed frames at Goodwill. Last night, they'd bought sheet sets, pillows, mattress covers, and blankets at Kmart. Early this morning, they'd washed away the newness from the sheets and blankets and hung them to dry.

Jas went into the closet-sized room that would be hers. The bed was pushed into the corner, leaving a foot of space on two sides. The new bedcovers were neatly folded and stacked in the middle. Sitting down, she bounced on the mattress. It was springy, and when she held the blanket to her nose and breathed deeply, it smelled like fresh air. At least she and Grandfather would sleep comfortably.

"Hello?" a cheery voice sang from outside. Jas leaped off the bed. Were Miss Tomlinson and Grandfather here already? Scurrying into the living room, she shoved the cleaning supplies and Shop-Vac out of sight in a closet.

"Yooo-hooo. Anyone home?" Jas recognized Mrs. Quincey's voice. The older woman had a heart of gold but was too wobbly around the rambunctious animals, so on some mornings she helped Miss Hahn with filing and phoning.

"In here, Mrs. Quincey." Jas opened the front door, which Rand had fixed this morning. Mrs. Quincey stood on the landing of the new steps. One hand clutched a flower-patterned throw pillow. The other clung tightly to the railing. Her gray hair was a halo of permed swirls. Her cheeks were powdered and rouged.

"Am I your first visitor?" she chirped.

"You are. Let me help you." Holding her elbow, Jas steered her into the living room.

"This is lovely!" Mrs. Quincey beamed at the bare space.

"It will be."

"Yesterday, I moved into assisted living. One bedroom—can you imagine?" She tottered into the kitchen, opening and shutting the cupboard doors.

"Thank you for everything you sent us," Jas said. "See how nicely it all fits?" She gestured to the shelves stacked with the blue-rimmed china.

"I'm so glad you and Karl can use it."

"Karl?"

"Didn't your grandfather tell you we were friends?"

Jas's brows rose. "No."

"I was in the nursing home for a week recovering from hip surgery while he was there. We hit it off. After I was discharged, I kept visiting him." She lowered her voice as if confiding in Jas before adding, "Such a gentleman."

"Grandfather?" Jas pictured his callused fingers and manure-stained overalls.

"He's a peach." Mrs. Quincey handed her the pillow. "This is for your sofa, dear."

"Thank you." She hugged it to her chest, still wondering about Grandfather and Mrs. Quincey.

Were they an item, as her grandmother used to say? "We don't have a sofa yet. But when we do, this will look beautiful on it."

"Of course it will." Mrs. Quincey looked at Jas as if she was daft. "It matches perfectly."

A truck motor roared outside. "Is someone waiting for you?" Jas asked, knowing the older woman never could have climbed the path. Then she heard voices and a rap on the door. When Jas opened it, Miss Hahn grinned at her from behind a lamp shade. Behind her, a line of people snaked down the steps and alongside the front of the mobile home. Mr. Muggins and another volunteer named George had a rolled rug draped over their shoulders. Lucy and her mother each carried a kitchen chair. Others carried a round wood table, a bedside table, and a stand lamp. At the end of the line, Chase and Rand held opposite ends of a flowered sofa that matched the pillow.

Jas burst into tears. Covering her face, she retreated into the living room. As Miss Hahn passed by, she handed her a tissue and whispered, "The investigator will be here tomorrow morning." Nodding, Jas blew her nose, overwhelmed by everyone's kindness.

Mrs. Quincey patted her shoulder. "Go

ahead, dear. I cried, too, when I moved into my new apartment."

"Is this all from your old house?" Jas waved at the growing pile.

"Yes, and I'm so pleased you can use it. My belongings will have a happy home here."

"Where do you want the sofa?" Rand hollered from the doorway.

"Against this wall." Mrs. Quincey directed with moving-man firmness. "But first we need to put down the carpet. Mr. Muggins, George!" She gestured for them to hurry over. Jas helped roll out the rug. It was cornflower blue with a plush pile. "Don't tear the sofa cover, gentlemen," Mrs. Quincey scolded as Chase and Rand staggered over under the weight.

Half an hour later, the volunteers were gone. Jas couldn't believe the transformation. And when Grandfather arrived with Miss Tomlinson, she greeted him with a hug and said, "We're finally home."

As she showed him around, he silently inspected each room. Then, pale and shaky, he sank into a recliner. Patting the overstuffed arm, he whispered, "Mine."

Miss Tomlinson gave her instructions about Grandfather's medications before leaving. Jas thanked her for all her help and then perched on the arm of the chair. Grandfather's eyes were closed. His lower jaw sagged with approaching sleep.

"Grandfather." She rubbed his wrist. It was cool to the touch despite the summer heat. "Before you take a nap, I need to ask you about Tommy Looney."

"'ooney?" He forced his eyes open. "I know 'at name."

"He was the one who hauled Whirlwind the day she left High Meadows."

"He 'id?" His gray eyes shifted to meet hers.

"Yes. Of course, he denied it. *But I know.*" She said it with such conviction that Grandfather bobbed his head. "What I don't know is how we can get more information out of him. We need to find out where he took her."

Grandfather ran his hand down his face. His fingers made a scratching noise as they passed over his whiskers. For the first time, Jas wondered if she would be able to care for him. The nurse's assistants had helped him bathe and shave. Would she have to take over those tasks? No one had told her.

Taking Jas's hand, Grandfather pressed it

between his. "Don't mess with Tommy 'ooney," he told her. "You'll scare 'im away if you start asking questions."

She bit her lip. "I was afraid you'd say that. The investigator from the insurance agency is coming tomorrow morning."

"Let 'im 'andle it," he said.

Jas blew out an impatient breath, tired of waiting for others to get the job done. "Okay, but how about if—"

Grandfather gripped her hand hard, cutting off her words. "Stay 'way from 'ooney. He's cagey. Smart. Like Hugh." A troubled look came over his face.

Jas swallowed hard. Tommy Looney must be "cut from the same cloth," as her grandmother used to say.

"Promise me," he said, his voice fading as he grew tired.

"I promise."

Grandfather sighed deeply as if satisfied. Then his lids grew heavy, his grasp loosened, and his chin dropped to his chest as he fell asleep.

Silence filled the mobile home. Jas shivered as she tried to picture Tommy Looney. She must have seen him at High Meadows. But she couldn't conjure a face. All she knew was that he was the person who had driven Whirlwind from the farm and from her life.

Now he would be the one who would help bring her back.

Twelve

⚜   ⚜   ⚜

JAS AIMED THE NOZZLE OF THE HOSE AT Shadow. She'd ridden him that morning, and his neck and back were streaked with sweat. As she sprayed, he danced and bit at the stream of water as if she hadn't trotted him for two hours. She, on the other hand, was exhausted. By the end of the ride, her legs had felt like jelly.

"Stand!" Jas commanded, to no avail. She wanted him bathed and cooled before the investigator showed up. M. Baylor hadn't given Miss Hahn a definite time. Jas was expecting the investigator any minute.

The phone conversation with Tommy Looney played again through her mind. She was sure he could lead her to Whirlwind. Before talking to him, she'd been impatient. Now she was bursting.

From the corner of her eye, Jas spotted Miss Hahn coming from the backyard of the house. Walking with her was a young woman, petite next to Miss Hahn's large frame. As Jas wiped Shadow's face with a towel, she watched them approach. Miss Hahn wore khaki shorts, a baggy T-shirt, and Muck Boots. The visitor wore a tight black skirt, a fitted sleeveless blouse, and strappy sandals. Gold bracelets ringed her arms. Her hair had chunky blond highlights and was stylishly cut with sweeping bangs, as if she was a Hollywood celebrity.

The woman was obviously not a volunteer. A rich donor? Jas guessed. Miss Hahn was always hitting up "society" ladies for contributions.

Jas draped the towel over her shoulder and turned out Shadow in the paddock. He immediately rolled, kicking his legs in the air. When he was thoroughly coated with dirt, he scrambled to his feet and shook like a dog.

"Jas, I'd like you to meet Marietta Baylor, the insurance investigator," Miss Hahn said when they came up to where Jas stood by the gate.

Jas studied the woman with raised brows. Her makeup was flawless. Despite the heat, there wasn't a glimmer of sweat or a hair out of place. Her clothes obviously came from a high-end boutique and not Wal-Mart. So how in the world was *this* Lucy clone going to help them? By shopping Hugh to death? Threatening him with her manicured fingernails?

"Nice to meet you." Ms. Baylor firmly shook Jas's hand. With each shake, her bracelets jangled. "I've heard all about your intriguing case, and I'm eager to get started."

"Get started doing what? Accessorizing?" Jas pulled her palm from the woman's grasp. "This isn't *The Case of the Missing Celebrity,* Ms. Baylor. We're searching for a horse, which means stomping through manure and flies, not waltzing down the red carpet." She knew she was being rude, but after all this waiting, her patience was thin.

"Jas, that was not necessary," Miss Hahn said sharply

Ms. Baylor smiled. "Don't worry. I get that reaction a lot. No one expects a female investigator in heels. But you know the old saying, 'You can catch more flies with honey than vinegar.' That especially holds true in the so-called genteel society of the horse world."

Crossing her arms, Jas listened, slightly intrigued. Along with her beauty, the woman had killer calf muscles and biceps. Thank goodness Chase wasn't here. His tongue would be hanging. But mostly Jas listened because right now, M. Baylor was her best chance for finding Whirlwind.

"Hugh Robicheaux and his cohorts are not going to be fooled by an investigator wearing a Sam Spade fedora," the investigator went on. "I need to blend in."

"Only, women like you don't 'blend in' with rednecks like Tommy Looney," Jas pointed out curtly.

Smiling slyly, Ms. Baylor unbuttoned her two top buttons. Then she moistened her lips and artfully mussed her hair. "Hey, fellas," she drawled. Arching her back, she thrust out her chest. "Y'all want another beer?"

The transformation from elegant lady to sexy waitress was so amazing that Jas let out a startled laugh.

"Well," Miss Hahn said, impressed. "You are quite the chameleon."

"I need to be in this business." Ms. Baylor rebuttoned her blouse. "Now, let's get down to the reason I'm here: finding Whirlwind. The insurance company needs the mare in order to win the case against Hugh."

Miss Hahn led the way into the office trailer. Mrs. Quincey was filing paperwork in the high cabinet. Half-glasses were perched on her nose.

"Why, hello," she greeted, eyeing the newcomer.

"Thank you, Mrs. Quincey," Miss Hahn said as she cleared file folders and unpaid bills off chair seats. "You've done enough for one day. You were wonderful help."

"I did clear one spot on your desk." Mrs. Quincey smiled cheerily. "Well, I believe I'll go visit with your grandfather, Jas."

"He'd love to see you. He's been grumbling all morning about not having enough to do."

"I'll take care of that. Good day, ladies," Mrs. Quincey said crisply as if slightly miffed that no one had introduced her. Jas helped her down the stairs. After she shut the door, she slid the list of dealers and the scrap of paper with the names of haulers from her back pocket. "Tommy Looney is our best lead to

Whirlwind," Jas said, handing the papers to Ms. Baylor, who sat down on one of the chairs.

The investigator crossed her tan legs. Pulling reading glasses from her purse, she slid them on and read the lists while murmuring *hmmms* and *uh-huhs*. Jas leaned against a desk and fiddled with a pen, too nervous to sit.

"I recognize all the agents," Ms. Baylor said. "Scott Black and Jenny Ferraro buy and sell horses up and down the East Coast. I've never heard any complaints about them. Anthony Bixby and Rose McDonough, however, sell horses internationally."

"Dr. Danvers and I talked about the possibility that Whirlwind could have been sold overseas," Jas said.

"Where she'll be tough to trace," Ms. Baylor said.

At least she didn't say impossible *to trace*. Miss Hahn put her arm around Jas's waist and squeezed comfortingly. But the investigator wasn't saying anything Jas didn't already know.

"I know most of the haulers on your list, too. Except for Tommy Looney. He must be strictly local. Which was smart of Hugh if he did hire the man. May I keep these for my file?"

Miss Hahn nodded. "I made copies."

Ms. Baylor slid the papers into her purse. Pulling out a BlackBerry, she faced Jas. "Now tell me about your phone conversation with Mr. Looney."

Jas repeated it word for word, adding, "Grandfather said he lives in Craigsville on Oak Mountain Road in a house trailer. He's got a big rig parked in the front yard."

While Jas talked, Ms. Baylor entered the information into her BlackBerry. "Did your grandfather say where Looney hangs out?"

"At Big Mama's Bar and Café."

Miss Hahn gave directions to the popular watering hole. "Be careful if you go there alone," she cautioned.

Ms. Baylor's smile was as sugary as a Southern belle's. "Honey, don't worry about me." Before Jas could blink, the investigator slipped a knife from somewhere. Holding it in under the throat of a pretend assailant, she said coolly, "I've handled all shapes and sizes. From brawny truck drivers to bald businessmen."

Miss Hahn chuckled. "Yes, I believe you can handle any situation."

"But thanks for the warning about Big Mama's." Just as magically, the knife disappeared and Ms. Baylor's professional manner returned. "Now, I need a photo of Whirlwind for identification."

Jas slid the worn picture from her back pocket. Her heart twisted as she handed it to the investigator. She hated giving up her only photo. But that wasn't the only reason she felt messed up inside. *Finally* something was happening. But what if it wasn't enough? What if it didn't work? What if the investigator came up with nothing?

"This is a good photo," Ms. Baylor said. "The irregular star and three white socks are clear. So unless the new owner has dyed her markings, she'll be easy to identify."

"Whirlwind also has a scar under her forelock near the crown," Jas said. "When she was a yearling, she reared in a horse trailer and needed stitches. Dr. Danvers should have a record of it."

"I'll check with him." Ms. Baylor stood up. "Thank you both for your help. I'll contact you as soon as I find out something."

Jas slid off the desk, her anxiety rising. "That's it? That's all you want from us—from me? Can't I help in some way? Can't I go with you?"

Ms. Baylor tilted her head as she hooked her purse strap over her shoulder. "I understand your impatience, Jas. You want Whirlwind found immediately. However, investigations usually take months."

"Months?" Jas sucked in a breath.

"Scam artists like Hugh Robicheaux are careful and clever. We just recently shut down a scheme where racehorses were being sold for inflated prices. An agent and appraiser were both in on it. Before a sale, the appraiser would place a high value on a horse, even though the actual money changing hands between the previous owner and the new owner was way lower. Based on the appraiser's value, the new owner could insure the horse for the inflated price. If the horse injured itself on the track or proved not to be a winner, it was killed."

Miss Hahn shook her head sadly. "It's bad enough that horses are dying from neglect. I didn't realize that killing them for profit was so common."

"Not common. But money does corrupt.

Fortunately, when we arrested the agent, he implicated the others. Still, even with all the evidence, it took us two years to get a conviction."

"Two *years*?" Jas repeated, horrified.

"You've given me good information on how to find Tommy Looney," Ms. Baylor said. "He may be gullible enough to spill the beans after a wink and a beer. Or it could take weeks of earning his confidence. That's the reality, Jas. In the meantime, I'll also be checking the agents' records for any suspicious transactions."

"You can do that?" Miss Hahn asked. "Legally?"

Ms. Baylor only smiled. "As for you, Jas, pack a bag. When I find Whirlwind, I'll need you to identify her right away, even if she's as far away as California. And I don't need to tell you both"—she looked from Jas to Miss Hahn, her expression grave—"that everything we've talked about remains confidential."

Jas opened her mouth. Should she tell Ms. Baylor that someone might be leaking information to Hugh? She had no proof, and since that day at the courthouse, Hugh hadn't contacted her. Plus, other than her own paranoia, there hadn't been any real evidence that someone was spying.

Turning, Ms. Baylor opened the office door. Heckle and Jeckle stood on the top step. When they saw the visitor, they brayed loudly. Most people shrieked with surprise when the two burros greeted them, but Ms. Baylor calmly scratched their fuzzy necks and cooed, "Hello, loves. Aren't you the cutest things?"

"You mean the most annoying things." Jas shooed them off the stairs.

Ms. Baylor handed her a business card. "Call my cell any time."

"Thank you." Jas tucked it in the pocket of her jeans. "For everything," she added, meaning it. Her first reaction to the woman had completely changed. She was glad Ms. Baylor was on her side.

At the bottom of the steps, the investigator paused and looked up at Jas. "I need to caution you. If Hugh Robicheaux finds out we're looking for Whirlwind, there's no telling what he'll do."

"Oh, I know what he'll do." Jas narrowed

her eyes. "Any person who can kill a horse for money has no soul. No conscience. Which means Hugh Robicheaux won't hesitate to kill a person—especially one who gets in his way. Like *me*."

Thirteen

❖　❖　❖

LIKE ME. JAS COULDN'T GET THE TWO WORDS out of her head. She'd spit them out like a dare, hoping Ms. Baylor wouldn't see how afraid she was. But, really, Hugh scared her.

She was huddled in the clean straw in a corner of Shadow's stall. The barn's ceiling fans rotated, stirring the hot air and keeping the flies away. Beside her, Shadow chewed contentedly on a flake of hay.

Like me. Jas had lived at High Meadows Farm since she was nine. She'd worked with Hugh almost every day. Yet she knew in her heart that he wouldn't hesitate to kill her if he found out she was still looking for Whirlwind.

Closing her eyes, she pictured her old life. Grandfather had always worked on horse farms, so Jas had been riding since she could walk. But Hugh was the first to notice her talent. Taking her under his wing, he'd instructed her every day. Not only did she love the hours of riding, but also she was a natural. It wasn't long before the horses she rode won classes, then championships. Soon he'd called her his protégé. Soon he'd loved her.

Or so she'd thought.

But Hugh loved only Hugh. She'd been a pawn. "Great job!" he'd tell her, but his praise was always followed by "You bring out the best in Hero"—or Blossom or Raisin or whatever horse she was riding.

His praise had seduced her into thinking he cared about her. But really, the only thing he'd cared about was that she made his horses shine in the ring and in front of clients. Her talent sold horses. It made him money.

And it had been a curse. Like Chase had said, she'd been on her way to becoming a mini Hugh.

Thank goodness for Second Chance Farm. She glanced up at Shadow. He gazed at her with big brown eyes, a hunk of hay sticking from his mouth. Whirlwind's "death," the farm, and especially riding Shadow had saved her.

Drawing up her knees, Jas wrapped her arms around them. Shadow bent down and blew at her hair. She reached up and stroked the white stripe that ended with a dot. "Thank you, buddy," she whispered. "For helping me break the curse."

Outside, a car door slammed. Jas startled, banging her head against the stall wall. Wincing, she rubbed the bump already forming. No wonder she was jumpy. Ever since meeting Hugh in the courthouse, she'd felt his eyes peering from every dark corner. Felt his fingers squeezing her neck.

Rubbing her throat, she tried to erase him from her mind. He was still after her, that she knew.

It was stupid of her not to have said something to Ms. Baylor. Maybe Hugh hadn't acted on his threats, but that didn't mean he wouldn't.

Chase's voice came from outside. It was late afternoon, time to turn out the horses. He was talking to George about which horse went in which pasture.

Jas held her breath as the two came into the barn. She didn't want to see George or Chase. She wanted to stay hidden in the stall, Shadow's bulk safely between her and the door. Because, if she was honest with herself, Hugh wasn't the only thing she was worried about. Last night, she'd helped Grandfather change into his pajamas. It had taken forever—he'd insisted he could do it himself, yet couldn't. And she'd been all thumbs. Finally they'd given up on his buttons and he'd slept in his cotton T-shirt. By then, he'd been so exhausted and Jas so frustrated she'd forgotten about helping him wash his hands and brush his teeth.

Then this morning, when she went in to wake him, he was lying so still she'd thought he was dead. No, worse than dead: paralyzed and unable to care for himself for the rest of his life. Fortunately, he'd only been sound asleep. But guilt had instantly swept over her. What kind of granddaughter was she? Grandfather had taken care of her for fourteen years. He'd nursed Grandmother when she was sick. Couldn't she lovingly do the same for him?

Except if he couldn't work at Second Chance Farm, what would happen to them? What would happen if he had another stroke? Miss Hahn couldn't afford to keep them on as charity cases. Jas wouldn't stand for that, anyway. It had been bad enough being a foster kid.

"Hiding?" someone asked.

Jas jumped as if Hugh had opened the stall door, knife in hand, instead of Chase carrying a lead line.

"I didn't know I was that terrifying," he said.

"You could have warned me," she snapped as she pushed herself to her feet, angry for being so skittish.

"It's not like I was sneaking around." He pointed a thumb down the aisle. "You didn't hear me cussing up a storm? George left the supply room door open, and Rose snuck in and tore open a feedbag."

"No, I didn't." Grabbing the end of the lead line, she tugged on it. "*I'll* turn Shadow out."

"You don't need to bite my head off." He tugged back.

Jas bristled. "Are you talking to me or Shadow?" She yanked harder.

Chase studied her hand on the rope; her knuckles were white. "Are you looking for a fight?"

"No." Stepping back, she let go. "Sorry."

"Sure you are." He tossed the lead line at her and strode from the stall.

Jas kicked Shadow's bucket. *Darn, darn, darn. Why do I do that?* Hooking the lead onto Shadow's halter, she hurried after Chase, who was leading Jinx from the barn. Outside the door, Hope was curled in a pile of raked up straw. Jas almost tripped over her. Shadow missed her tail by an inch. The little dog didn't budge.

"Chase? Wait." She caught up to him at the pasture gate. He'd already turned out Jinx, who was trotting off.

"I didn't mean to yell at you," Jas said as she led Shadow into the pasture. "It's just that—"

Shadow reared back, eager to be with Jinx. The lead line ripped through her fingers. He raced after Jinx, the rope flapping. "Shoot!" she swore as she ran after him, hollering, "Whoa! Whoa!" But he flew down the hill, out of sight.

Stopping, she blew out a frustrated breath. There was no use chasing him. He'd think it was a game of tag that he wasn't going to lose.

She turned. Chase was leaning back against the closed gate. His arms were loosely crossed. His grin was crooked and, she thought, a little sad.

Jas strolled over, fingers shoved in her front pockets. His grin widened as if he'd shaken off the hurt. "What's so funny?" she asked.

"You are, horse girl." Chase jutted his chin

toward Jinx and Shadow, who had stopped to graze at the farthest possible spot. "You handle *Equus caballus* as well as you handle *homo sapiens*."

"Look who's flinging out scientific words to impress."

"No need to impress someone who's already doing a good job of screwing up."

Her mouth fell open. "That was a mean thing to say."

"You deserve it."

"All right. I do." Jas flopped back next to him. "I had an attack of the Hughs. I'm sorry. I know that's no excuse for snapping at you. But I keep expecting him to pop up, match in hand, and burn down the barn." She frowned. "Why *isn't* he skulking around trying to destroy us?"

"How do you know he's not?"

"I don't. That's what's so freaky." She shuddered, suppressing the urge to glance over her shoulder.

"Let's hope he's lying low, letting his lawyers do the dirty work," Chase said.

She rubbed her bare arms, which prickled with goose bumps as if it was a winter day. "No. He's planning something. I can feel it."

Just then, Shadow came thundering over the hill. He slid to an ungainly halt in front of her. His nostrils flared and he puffed dramatically.

Reaching up, Jas unsnapped the lead line. "Thanks for not killing yourself, dummy." She gave him a quick pat before he wheeled and raced off again.

As she stood there, she could feel Chase's eyes on her. Self-conscious, she scraped the toe of her sneaker in the dirt. When she realized she was outlining a heart, she panicked and scuffed it out.

Still he didn't say anything. What was he thinking? Was he still mad? Jas wouldn't blame him. She had no right to be mean to her friends. Make that *friend,* singular. Chase was her only real friend.

That's not true. Miss Hahn, Dr. Danvers, Grandfather—all three had stuck by her through this mess. Still, they weren't Chase.

Jas glanced sideways at him. He was still watching her, his gaze intense. As if he could see into her heart. As if he knew how scared she was.

"What?" she asked, wanting to sound tough, but it came out in a whisper. She cleared her throat, her pulse beating fast. His eyes were crystal blue and his smile breathtaking. *No fair,* she wanted to tell him. *Stop making me like you.*

Then he shrugged, his reply to her question. She swallowed hard, trying not to look away. But her insides were fluttering, and she flicked her gaze back to the horses.

"I was just wondering," he finally said. Straightening, he turned and lifted the gate latch.

Wondering what? Wondering if I like you?

"If I were James Bond"—he held open the gate for Jas—"and Hugh was Goldfinger, how would I take him out? Bomb his Mercedes? Poison his scotch?"

She stopped in her tracks. Here she'd been resisting acting like a lovesick fool and he'd been channeling James Bond. "Only you're *not.*" She punched him on the shoulder. "And Hugh is a real villain, not some movie actor. So come on. We've got a barn full of horses to turn out. And when we're done with the horses, let's take Hope back to her old home. I'm tired of seeing her moping around. We need to find her friend."

She strode brusquely toward the barn, all thoughts of romance gone. *Guys are so clueless.* But then she realized her step was lighter.

Lucy came out of the barn, leading Flower. When they passed each other, she said, "Hey, Jas, who was the lady I saw you talking to? The one wearing Jimmy Choos?"

Jas felt a prickle of apprehension. Why was Lucy interested in Ms. Baylor?

"What's a Jimmy Choo?" Chase asked.

"She's just some filthy-rich donor that Miss Hahn is courting," Jas said quickly. "Come on, Chase, we've got to feed Rose before she busts down the fence." Linking her arm through his, she pulled him into the barn.

He stopped in front of the supply room. "What was that all about?"

"About Lucy being too nosey." Jas unbolted the door.

"You can't possibly think that Lucy . . ." He burst into guffaws. "Right—the Mata Hari of the cheerleaders."

Jas shot him an annoyed look. "I'm just being careful, okay? Even the investigator, Ms. Baylor, said to be cautious. She's worried Hugh will find out, too. And you have to admit, Lucy's spending a lot of time on Mill Road with all the rich folks. Maybe she really *has* gone to the dark side."

"*Lucy?* She's more *Gossip Girl* than *Goldfinger.*"

"You know, Chase, the James Bond stuff is getting really lame. So quit." Flinging open the door, Jas scooted inside. "I'll feed the chickens. You feed Rose." She pulled the top off a feed tub and began scooping cracked corn into a bucket. When Chase didn't say anything, she glanced over her shoulder.

The doorway was empty. Straightening, she listened. No whistle, country song, or corny jokes came from the aisle, either.

Jas wanted to kick herself. She'd acted like an idiot again. If only she could make Chase understand that it wasn't *him;* it was the worry. Grandfather, Hugh, the farm, Whirlwind. It was eating her up inside.

And not even James Bond could help.

Fourteen

❖ ❖ ❖

"DONATIONS ARE WAY DOWN," MISS HAHN TOLD the circle of volunteers who were gathered in her living room that evening. She was seated in the rocking chair, a ledger and file folder on her lap. To her right, Lucy and Chase sat on the floor on either side of an open pizza box. Rand, Mr. Muggins, and Dr. Danvers were lined up on the sofa, pizza slices in hand as they ate. Grandfather sat on a love seat.

Jas was hunched on the footstool, her chin propped on her bent palm. "Pizza?" Chase offered. She hoped it meant he'd forgiven her for her earlier bad mood.

"No thanks," she said. Miss Hahn had told her what this meeting was about, and it had ruined her appetite.

"We're spending twice as much for hay," Miss Hahn went on. "The grass isn't growing in the pastures. No one's adopting—folks can barely afford their own animals. So right now, we have too many mouths to feed."

"What about your big donors? Clark's Feed, Tom's Grocery, and Stanford Hardware?" Dr. Danvers asked. "They've been regulars for years."

Miss Hahn glanced at the open ledger in her lap. She tucked a graying strand of hair behind her ear and then looked up. Her whole face sagged.

Jas knotted her fingers. She'd never seen Miss Hahn so upset. So defeated. Usually her former foster mom was a bundle of optimism. She had learned to stay positive in order to handle case after case of abuse.

"They've suddenly chosen not to support us," Miss Hahn said quietly. "And today when I called the Stanford Grill, they told me they were withdrawing support as well."

Murmurs of disbelief rose in the room. But Jas wasn't surprised. This was Hugh's way of retaliating, she bet. He'd discovered that the insurance company was going to prosecute. He knew they were looking for Whirlwind.

Jas crossed her arms over her stomach, the smell of the greasy pizza making her nauseous.

I can and I will destroy Diane and her precious farm. Hugh wasn't going to burn down a barn. He wasn't going after Jas with a knife. He was cutting off all donations. The farm and the animals she loved would never survive if funds dried up.

We can't let Hugh ruin us! Jas wanted to shout to the others. But who would believe it was his fault?

She listened to the conversations going on around her. Dr. Danvers and Grandfather were blaming the drop in donations on the slump in the economy. Miss Hahn and Mr. Muggins were blaming it on the drought and the price of feed. Jas swallowed a laugh. Not even the weather was as powerful as Hugh.

Okay, a foolish exaggeration. But Jas had lived at High Meadows farm for four years. She'd witnessed the influence he had in Stanford. His relatives, friends, and employees shopped at Tom's Grocery and Stanford Hardware. They dined at the Stanford Grill and bought their feed from Clark's. Jas couldn't blame the businesses for stopping their donations. They couldn't afford to alienate Hugh.

The voices grew heated as suggestions and accusations flew. Jas wanted to plug her ears.

She wanted to flee from the room. Instead, she sat frozen on the footstool. *No more running away.*

Suddenly, Chase dropped down beside her, bumping her with his hip. "Scoot over."

"There's no room," she said as she slid toward the edge.

"There's room." He stuck his long legs in front of him. Pizza sauce dotted his lower lip. Jas pointed it out and he licked it off with a dart of his tongue.

"Sorry about this afternoon," she apologized.

He shrugged. "No problem." Leaning closer, he whispered, "Hey, you don't think—"

"Ugh." Jas fanned the air. "Garlic breath."

"I swear." With a roll of his eyes, he pulled a pack of gum from his pocket. "I knew *Lucy* was a princess." He popped a piece in his mouth and chewed noisily. "Better?"

She nodded.

"Okay, back to my question. You think Hugh's behind the donation fiasco, don't you?"

Jas stared at him. "Are you serious?"

"Why wouldn't I be?"

"Because I thought . . ."

"No one would believe you?"

"Exactly."

"Let's find out." Chase leaped up, his lanky frame towering over those who were seated. Putting two fingers in his mouth, he whistled shrilly. When the others stopped talking, he said, "Jas and I think Hugh is behind the drop in donations. It makes sense. Four businesses stopping their donations in one week is too much of a coincidence."

Jas glanced around, noticing a lot of dubious expressions.

"We all know the Robicheauxs have a lot of influence in town," Chase continued. "Hugh might be getting back at Jas for . . ."

Jas tugged on his pant leg, warning him not to blab too much.

". . . finding out about Shadow being Aladdin."

"That makes no sense," Dr. Danvers said. "Someone in Hugh's position hires powerful lawyers to win his fights for him."

"Really," Lucy said. "I work for Mrs. Vandevender. She has good things to say about Hugh. And she's nice. All rich people aren't snotty and cruel."

Chase's neck reddened and he abruptly sat

down. "Thanks for trying," Jas whispered. "I don't deserve such a great friend."

He grinned. "You're right."

Grandfather rapped his cane on the floor. "I agree with 'ase and Jas," he declared. "Hugh is a sneaky snake."

Jas gave him a grateful look.

"Well, we already know he's hired top-notch lawyers," Miss Hahn said. "And the kids are right: Hugh will stop at nothing· to win. However, the truth of the matter is that the farm is running out of money. The reason doesn't matter. We have one month of operating budget left. After that . . ." She faltered.

Jas held her breath. The "after that" was too horrible to think about.

Miss Hahn cleared her throat. Her eyes were red-rimmed. "After that, we'll have to surrender the animals to other shelters and farms."

"No!" the cry burst out before Jas could stop it. All eyes swung to her. She shut her mouth, hesitating when she realized the others were waiting for her to speak. Then she straightened her spine. She was tired of being scared. Tired of running away.

"I'm not going to let this farm be destroyed," she said. "Miss Hahn said we have a month. That's enough time to raise more money. I saw how everyone pitched in to make a home for Grandfather and me. We can use that energy to make sure our animals don't have to leave the farm unless they've found a better home."

"I second the motion," Chase said. "School doesn't start for three weeks. That's three weeks to bake cookies and wash cars and do whatever we have to do to raise money."

Rand, who'd mostly been silent, said, "I've been thinkin'. We need to fence in those five acres on the other side of the pond. There's good grass there."

"Only we can't afford fencing materials," Miss Hahn pointed out.

"Electric wire's cheap enough," Mr. Muggins said.

"But so tacky." Lucy scrunched her nose. Jas flinched as she remembered saying the same thing not so long ago. "Mrs. Vandevender is replacing her wooden fence with that fancy vinyl stuff. I bet she'd give us the old boards and posts."

"Good, good." Miss Hahn began furiously writing on a piece of paper in the folder. Jas let out a relieved breath. She felt Chase's palm brush against hers. Slowly, their fingers entwined.

Jas felt herself relax against him—as if his hand holding hers meant that everything would be all right. She stole a quick glance at him. When he smiled, her heart did a little flip.

This time she didn't draw away. This time she told herself that being close to Chase felt just right.

And as the energy and ideas filled the room, she also knew that this was one fight they were going to win.

Early the next morning, Jas and Chase strode down the drive to Hope's old home, the pup trotting beside them on a leash. Officer Lacey had given up on the Havahart trap after catching a slew of possums and raccoons. Jas, however, was determined to find Hope's friend. She knew what it was like to feel lost and alone.

Okay, so maybe she was putting her own feelings onto the dog. But one more thing she'd learned at Second Chance Farm was that animals had emotions, too.

As they walked, Jas and Chase discussed possible designs for a brochure to mail out for raising funds. Chase had taken a course on Microsoft Publisher. Lucy had a digital camera. All they needed was time to put it together.

When the brick ranch house came into view, Jas slowed. A sign for an upcoming auction was tacked to the front door. Officer Lacey had told them the place was empty. Still, tire tracks were tamped in the lawn as if someone had driven right up to the door. A windowpane was broken. A chair with three legs lay upended on the steps.

"Looks like someone ransacked the place," Chase said.

"Maybe they were looking for drugs." Jas shivered. The place was as silent and eerie as a cemetery.

Tugging on the leash, Hope whined. Her nose quivered. Her eyes were alert under her tufts of hair. "She senses something," Jas said.

"Her phantom friend?" Chase wasn't as convinced as Jas.

"Come on, Double-o-seven, let's put your sleuthing skills to good use."

"I don't remember James ever tracking missing canines." But he followed her past the house to the backyard. Jas stepped over a ripped garbage bag, its contents spilled and blown across the unmowed lawn. Paint cans and a rusted ladder had been tossed in front of the garage doorway.

"Looks like someone is using this place for a dump, too." She pointed into the garage's shadowy interior. "That's where Hope was chained. No food or water."

Chase stepped inside to look around. Hope cowered at Jas's feet, trembling. She leaned over and stroked her furry head. "Don't worry. You're not going in there."

"Creepy," Chase said when he came out a second later. "Like the torture chamber in a horror movie. How could a person do that to his dog?"

"To *two* dogs."

"You're right. It does look as if there were two dogs. But that doesn't mean it's still around. Look at Hope." The pup was pressed against Jas's ankle. "If you let her go, she'd be out of here in a flash. Maybe her friend found a new home, too."

"I doubt it." Walking Hope around the sagging outbuildings, Jas called, "Here, boy. Here, doggie." When she returned to where Chase was still standing, she sighed. "No sign of it."

"Let's think positively." Chase started back

toward the driveway. "And imagine it's curled on a pillow in some cushy house."

Hope trotted after Chase as if just as eager to get away. Then suddenly she whirled. Ears pricked, she stared into the thick brush beyond the garage. She quivered—with fear? Joy? Jas couldn't tell.

"Chase," she called over her shoulder. "Hope sees something."

Then branches snapped and Hope began to bark. She strained at the leash. Goose bumps prickled Jas's arms. "Chase!"

He jogged back. "What?"

"Something's in there." She waved toward the tangle of briars, orchard grass, and wild rose.

"A crazed drug dealer?"

"Whatever it is, it's big." Rustling sounds came from a blackberry thicket. "It *could* be Hope's missing friend," she said, trying to convince herself. "Here, girl! Here, boy!" she called. A grunting sound came from the thicket.

Chase grabbed her arm. "And it *could* be a bear having a morning snack of berries."

"A bear!" Jas had heard of bears in the area, though she'd never seen one.

Chase began to walk backward, pulling Jas

with him. "Don't run. Don't panic. Bears generally avoid people."

"Generally?"

"If they don't have cubs or are angry for some reason."

Still tugging on the leash, Hope barked louder. Jas scooped her up. "Shhh. It's okay, Hope. No need to bark."

Slowly they retreated. Jas stumbled over a paint can, but Chase kept her from falling. Then the grass and branches rustled and shook. Whatever it was, was heading toward them at a run.

"It's coming this way!" Jas cried the same instant a huge black creature burst from the undergrowth and lumbered straight for them.

Fifteen

❖ ❖ ❖

"RUN!" CHASE HOLLERED AS HE TOOK OFF. JAS stood motionless in fear. Hope dove from her arms and raced toward the charging creature. The tiny dog leaped in the air and began furiously licking its snout. Instantly the black beast flopped onto its back. Its paws flailed the air. Its tongue lolled in joy.

Jas gaped at the crazy sight. "It's a dog!" she exclaimed.

"A *what*?" Stopping, Chase stared in amazement, then jogged back.

The two dogs rolled on the grass, Hope whining and licking, the huge dog woofing and wiggling.

"It's a monster-sized one," Jas said. "A Newfoundland, maybe?"

"Looks like a Newfie. No wonder we thought it was a bear."

Letting out a giggle of relief, Jas nudged him in the side with her elbow. "Thank goodness you were here to save me, Double-o-seven," she teased.

"Don't mention it—*ever*." Reaching in his back pocket, Chase pulled out a dog cookie. "Let's see if the monster is friend or foe." Slowly, he approached, his eyes averted so as not to appear threatening. "Hey, boy."

"How do you know it's a boy?" Jas whispered, right behind him.

"I don't. But if it is a boy, I don't want to call him a girl and make him mad."

With a deep woof, the black dog suddenly scrambled to his feet. "Whoa!" Chase stopped so fast that Jas bumped into him. The dog launched in the air, knocking them both to the ground. It snatched the cookie from Chase's grasp, gulped it in one bite, then ran back to play with Hope.

Jas pushed herself up on one elbow. Chase was spread-eagled on the grass, blinking up at the sky as if dazed. She leaned over him, worried. "Are you all right?"

"Got the wind knocked out of me," he gasped. He tilted his head so he could see the two dogs. "So was that friend or foe?"

Jas laughed as she sat up. "Friend, I think. But if we bring him back to the farm, he might turn into foe." Drawing up her legs, she wrapped her arms around them and sighed. "Miss Hahn's not going to be happy with one more mouth to feed."

"And that's some mouth." Chase sat up next to her. "His coat's a wreck."

"And he's probably tick-infested." They groaned in unison at the thought of bathing such a big critter. "I wonder how he survived all this time."

"Maybe he caught mice? Rabbits?" Chase stood. "If we're going to get him home and cleaned up, we better get started." He held out his hand to her. Jas took it and he lifted her to her feet. His arm circled her waist, pulling her close. "I'd say this was quite the adventure," he said softly.

She nodded, her heart thumping faster than when she'd thought a bear was attacking. He bent his head. She tipped hers. All thoughts about Chase being only a friend vanished. Her eyes drifted shut and she held her breath. Their lips touched. Ever so lightly. And lingered until her mind grew dizzy.

"Nice," Chase whispered when he finally pulled back.

Very nice. Jas ducked her chin, too flustered to reply or even look at him. Her palm was pressed against his chest as if ready to push him away. Instead, she nodded in happy agreement.

Since yesterday, when they'd held hands, she'd felt a slight change in their relationship. The kiss had only heightened it.

She tilted her head, wanting him to kiss her again. But a giant mass of stinky fur barreled between them. "Hey!" They sprang apart. Rising up, the Newfie planted two paws on Chase's chest and slammed him again to the ground.

Jas burst out laughing as the dog licked Chase's face with a giant pink tongue. "I think you just made a new friend."

"Mrs. Quincey, this rum cake is to die for," Jas gushed. It was a week later. She, Chase, and Grandfather sat around the kitchen table in the mobile home. All three were sampling Mrs. Quincey's famous rum cake, soon to be featured in a fund-raising bake sale.

"You're right, dear, it *is* to die for," Mrs.

Quincey said. She was seated next to Grandfather, a red-plumed hat perched jauntily on her head. "It was Mr. Quincey's last dessert before his fatal heart attack."

Chase choked. Jas set down her fork. Grandfather asked for another piece.

Mrs. Quincey sliced into the golden bunt cake, drizzled with creamy, rum-flavored frosting. "He died with a smile on his face and crumbs on his lips."

"I believe it," Chase said. "I'd like another piece, too." He held out his plate.

Jas laughed and then said, "Thanks for organizing the bake sale, Mrs. Quincey. This cake will obviously be a hit."

"My pleasure. How are the other fundraising ideas going?" she asked as she served Chase and Grandfather a second piece.

"Terrific," Chase replied. "Mrs. Vandevender's employees delivered all the old fencing. She said she was glad to help."

"And we've mailed out almost two hundred brochures." Standing, Jas plucked one off the counter and handed it to the older woman. On the front was a photo of two horses taken the day they'd been rescued. Inside was a recent photo. "We sent them to businesses and organizations in other parts of the state."

Mrs. Quincey opened up the colorful brochure. "Very eye-catching and with a heartfelt message."

"Lucy had them printed—cheap," Chase said. "One of her 'boyfriends' works at the Copy Shop in Stanford. He gave her *quite* the deal in return for . . ." He waggled his eyebrows. Blushing, Jas looked away. When she dared to glance at him again, he was grinning as if he had a secret. She blushed harder as she thought about their kiss.

Jumping up, she took her plate to the sink. While the three talked about fund-raising, she washed her plate and stuck it in the dish drainer. The photos on the brochure were bound to attract attention from possible adopters. And Flower had been adopted by one of Dr. Danvers's clients. The young woman's own horse had foundered and had to be put down. Horse and human had been a perfect match.

Yes, lots had been done to save the farm. But *nothing* had been done to save Whirlwind. There'd been no word from Mr. Jenkins or Ms. Baylor all week. Every time Jas got near the office phone, her finger itched to call Tommy Looney. *Tell me where you hauled my horse!* But she didn't dare risk it.

Frustrated, Jas tackled the rust spots in the sink. Then she scrubbed the grime on the counter. Done with those tasks, she spun and began clearing the table. When she whisked the plate from under Grandfather's fork, he sputtered in protest.

"Let him finish eating, dear," Mrs. Quincey said in her syrupy voice.

Jas frowned. The woman was as syrupy as steel. She still hadn't figured out the relationship between her and Grandfather. The older lady had shown up every day since they'd moved in. She brought them homemade casseroles. She mended Grandfather's torn shirt. She read to him from the newspaper. She played pinochle with him.

She really seemed to care about him.

"Sorry." Jas set the plate down. She couldn't believe her minitirade. What was wrong with her? She should be glad for Mrs. Quincey's help. Caring for Grandfather this week had been challenging. Getting him dressed in the morning took forever. Sometimes, if Mrs. Quincey showed up early, Jas left. There was so much to do on the farm it was overwhelming. And she'd rather spend her time with Chase and Shadow and the other animals.

"I'm just in a hurry," Jas explained. "I want to ride before it gets too dark. Grandfather? More milk?"

"I'll get it, dear," Mrs. Quincey said. "You go ahead."

"I've gotta get going, too," Chase said. "Monster needs a walk before I head home." The Newfie had been named, bathed, and dipped and was almost finished with quarantine. Manners were another matter.

Standing, Chase stretched his arms over his head. "Plus I gotta get up early tomorrow," he continued. "Rand's making me dig post holes at dawn while it's not so blazing hot. My dad has a day off work, so he's helping."

Jas's ears pricked. Chase's dad had said there was nothing the Stanford Police Department could do about Hugh or Whirlwind. Still, he might have some suggestions. She was desperate for any help.

"I'll walk with you down the hill," Jas said to Chase. She plopped the sponge in the sink. "Will you guys be all right?" she asked, sounding like a parent talking to two teenagers.

Grandfather, finishing his cake, nodded. Mrs. Quincey made a shooing motion with her hand.

Jas grabbed her helmet from a peg on the wall and picked up her riding boots, which were by the door. Following Chase outside, she sat on the bottom step to put on her boots. Though it was still hot, the sun was sinking behind the mountains. A perfect time to ride.

"I feel porked out." Chase patted his stomach.

"Be glad that's all you feel. You heard Mrs. Quincey. That cake killed her husband."

"Must have been the rum. I feel a little loopy myself."

"Seriously, Chase." Bending, Jas tied her laces. "Don't you think it's weird she's hanging around all the time?"

"No. I think it's sweet."

"*Sweet?*" Jas plunked her booted foot on the ground.

"Yeah. They're like two lovebirds."

"Gross." She jumped up. "You're talking about old wrinkly people."

He arched one brow. "Old people can't fall in love?"

"Not when it's my grandfather. Can you

imagine? She'd be my stepgrandma. That's creepy."

He grinned as they started down the hill. "I think you're jealous."

She didn't disagree. "I'm wary. Maybe she's Hugh's spy."

Chase stopped dead, his mouth hanging open. "Mrs. Quincey? That's as crazy as suspecting Lucy."

"Yeah, you're right. Except she does hang around all the time."

"Because she likes your grandfather. I know the feeling." He took her hand in his. "You're sweet on my grandfather, too?" Jas teased.

"Absolutely." For a second, they grinned stupidly at each other before starting down the path, Chase walking in front. As the hill got steeper, he gained momentum. He broke into a jog, pulling Jas with him. "Actually, I think the spy is Rose," he said over his shoulder. "She's always watching us with those beady eyes. . . ."

Laughing, Jas hurtled after him. Since the day they'd found Monster, things had changed between them. All week, whenever she was around Chase, it felt as if her insides were humming. She loved the anticipation of seeing him. This new sensation was such a rush, she never wanted it to go away.

When they reached the front yard, they found Miss Hahn standing on the porch. A phone was in her hand. She waved urgently at Jas.

"It's Ms. Baylor," Miss Hahn said.

Letting go of Chase's hand, Jas ran to the porch. Taking the phone, she swung open the screen door and went into the living room. Her heart was thudding. "Hello?"

"Jas. I need your grandfather's help. I'd like him to go with me to talk to Tommy Looney."

"You found something out?"

"Not really. Looney is talking to me, but the man has two topics of conversation: NASCAR and his hound dog. Tomorrow night, I'm meeting Tommy at Big Mama's. I want your grandfather with me. I'm hoping since they know each other, he can weasel more information out of him."

"Of course. I'll tell him."

"I'll pick him up at nine o'clock."

"He'll be ready." Heart thumping, Jas pressed the OFF button. *And so will I.* There was no way she was going to miss talking to Tommy Looney. No way she was missing a chance to find out what happened to Whirl-wind.

"Chase! Miss Hahn! Finally something's happening!" Jas hollered. Pushing open the screen door, she burst outside, excited to share the news.

Sixteen

❖   ❖   ❖

JAS JIGGLED HER LEG. TAPPED HER LIP. PEERED out the window at Big Mama's. It was dark, and moths fluttered around the lone light above the bar's glass door. Flopping back against the car seat, she let out a frustrated breath. *What is taking them so long?!*

Grandfather and Ms. Baylor had been inside for half an hour. Ms. Baylor had warned Jas that it could take a while. She'd brought a book just in case and stayed hunched in the backseat, the car doors locked.

She was dying to go in after them. But a girl her age would attract too much attention. Tommy Looney could get suspicious. And she didn't want to distract the man from his purpose tonight: telling Grandfather where he'd hauled Whirlwind.

Still, waiting was frustrating. She glanced

again at the front of the building. On the concrete stoop, five bikers smoked and talked. Smoke clouded the air, and even though it had to be eighty degrees, they were all dressed in leather jackets.

Digging in her back pocket, Jas pulled out the piece of gum she'd swiped from Chase. He'd been mad that he couldn't come. After all, wasn't he James Bond? Jas had to remind him that, no, he wasn't. Now she wished he was here to keep her company. Except two teenagers hunkered in the backseat of a car . . .

Jas's face flamed. *I'm not going there,* she reminded herself as she stuck the gum in her mouth. But why had she finally let herself like Chase? From the moment she'd met him in Miss Hahn's kitchen, she'd felt something. And they'd always had fun together. Had she simply gotten tired of running away from her feelings?

The front door of Big Mama's swung open. Jas bolted upright. Grandfather hobbled out, followed by Ms. Baylor, who didn't look anything like M. Baylor, the investigator. Her black jeans and hot-pink tube top hugged every curve. Her chin-length hair was bleached sunbeam yellow and teased into a frothy dome.

Her lips and nails were ruby red, matching her cowboy boots.

Even Grandfather had been blinded by the outfit when she'd climbed from a Ford Escort sedan with chipped paint and bald tires. "A vehicle befittin' a gal down on her luck," Ms. Baylor had explained.

Taking a misstep, he'd stumbled over his own cane. And Chase had stammered, "Nice ta m-meet ya," as if he didn't have a brain in his head.

With frustrating slowness, Ms. Baylor escorted Grandfather out the door and through the bikers. Wolf whistles rang out. Grandfather whacked a biker's leg with his cane and barked, "Mind your manners, *boys*."

Jas cranked the handle to roll down the window, dying to find out what had happened, but the glass didn't move. Opening the door, she jumped out. "Well?" she asked impatiently as they crunched like turtles across the parking lot gravel.

Ms. Baylor shook her head. Jas opened the passenger side door. She took Grandfather's cane and, holding his elbow, helped him climb in. Grumbling under his breath, he lowered himself into the sunken seat. Jas lifted his right leg and tucked it inside. Then she laid his cane on his lap.

"'ooney wasn't there," Grandfather finally said. It was late, and his face looked drawn.

"What do you mean he wasn't there?" Jas looked over the top of the Ford at Ms. Baylor, who'd walked to the driver's side. "Wasn't he supposed to meet you?"

"Get in the car," she said, keeping her head down. "We don't need to attract any more attention than necessary."

Jas shut Grandfather's door and quickly jumped in the backseat.

"Tommy never showed," the investigator explained as she drove from Big Mama's lot.

Jas leaned forward so she could hear every detail. "Never showed?"

"Frank, the bartender, said Tommy had been at Big Mama's every night for weeks. He said not showing up wasn't like the guy."

Grandfather snapped his hand to indicate a left. "Turn 'ere on Oak Mountain to 'ooney's trailer."

Ms. Baylor slowed the car. "I'm not sure we should go to his place. I tried to call and didn't get an answer. It might seem odd if we just show up."

"Nah, 'ooney 'ill love an old friend coming by," Grandfather said.

"Yes, please let's go," Jas urged. "Maybe he was doing a hauling job and got delayed. Or NASCAR's on TV. Or his dog had a tick. We've got to see him tonight. The waiting is killing me."

The investigator flicked on the turn signal. "All right. But, Jas, you stay in the car."

"No way. Looney knows Grandfather has a granddaughter. He may even have seen me at High Meadows."

Ms. Baylor sighed, giving in. "Okay, but Looney thinks I'm Shasta, not Marietta. So don't slip up." She wagged a finger in Jas's direction. "And I'm warning you—he is either really dense or really cagey. So no blurting out questions about Whirlwind, got it?"

"Got it." As they drove down Oak Mountain Road, Jas chewed a nail in anticipation. Sweat dripped down her temples. "Doesn't the AC work?"

"Nope." Ms. Baylor rolled down the window. Steamy night air blew inside, bringing with it the sound of tree frogs. The car lights illuminated thick woods on both sides of the road. Jas didn't recognize the area but knew they were in the middle of nowhere.

"It's black as pitch out here," Ms. Baylor said. "I think your grandfather has fallen asleep. I need him to show me where Tommy lives."

"He's used to going to bed around nine." Reaching around the seat, Jas jiggled his shoulder. "Grandfather?" He woke with a snort. "Where's Tommy's house?" Jas asked. "We haven't seen any driveways."

"Huh? What?" Blinking sleepily, he stared at Ms. Baylor and then over his shoulder at Jas with a befuddled expression. She rubbed his shoulder. "Are you all right?"

He nodded but still looked confused. Jas wasn't sure if he knew where he was or who he was with, and it worried her.

"Grandfather, we're trying to find Tommy's trailer." As she explained again where they were going and why, his nods grew more vigorous. "'es, 'es. He lives down the 'oad." He waved Ms. Baylor ahead.

Jas blew out a relieved breath. He really was too old for all this intrigue. Maybe Chase should have come along.

"'ere! 'ere!" Grandfather flapped his hand to the right. Half hidden by weeds, a rusty mailbox on a post jutted from the middle of stacked truck tires.

"Nice outdoor decor," Ms. Baylor murmured as she turned down the rutted drive. Jas peered out the window. To the left, the headlights picked up the hulking form of a tractor trailer. Parked beside it was a horse van. Grass grew high around the tires of both vehicles, as if they hadn't been moved for a while. A trailer perched on concrete blocks stood at the end of the drive. Abandoned cars and lopsided stacks of firewood decorated the lawn.

Ms. Baylor parked and turned off the motor. A dim light shone in the house trailer. "Looks like he's home."

Jas opened her car door. A dog bayed. She hesitated, not sure where the sound was coming from. "'ooney's dog," Grandfather said. "He 'oves the flea-ridden critter."

Ms. Baylor made a noise of disgust. "I spent an entire evening listening to stories about that hound treeing raccoons. It was mind-numbing."

"What's its name?" Jas asked. "In case it comes to check us out."

"Digger," Ms. Baylor said. The hound bayed again.

" 'ooney keeps him tied up behind the trailer. Got a big dog 'ouse."

Jas climbed from the car and opened Grandfather's door. By then, Ms. Baylor had walked around to the passenger side.

Hands on her hips, the investigator studied the trailer. "That dog's really noisy. I'm surprised Looney isn't brandishing a shotgun out the window. He wasn't expecting visitors."

"That *is* weird," Jas agreed. At the farm, the dogs announced every arrival. There was no way a visitor or stranger could sneak up.

Holding Grandfather's arm, she hoisted him from the car. Ms. Baylor took his elbow on the other side, and together they got him square on his feet. For a moment he swayed. Then, using his cane, he headed toward the house.

The stairs to the front door were made of stacked concrete blocks. Stopping at the bottom, Grandfather grabbed Jas's arm for support. He rapped hard on the screen door with the tip of his cane and hollered, "'ooney! Tommy 'ooney!" The name echoed as if through an empty building. He rapped again, the aluminum door clanking loudly. Still no one responded.

The hound dog bayed, the sound rising gloomily into the night sky. Jas shivered. She hoped Ms. Baylor carried a weapon. Though where she would hide one in her skintight outfit was a mystery.

"Could be he's passed out drunk," Ms. Baylor said. "You two stay here. I'm going inside." Bending, she slid a small gun from her boot.

Jas kept hold of Grandfather. Ms. Baylor climbed the steps, arm relaxed by her side, the gun snug against her thigh. Opening the door, she stuck in her head and hollered, "Tommy! Hey, dude, it's Shasta. We missed you at Big Mama's."

When there was no answer, she went inside. The door crashed shut and Jas jumped. Leaves crackled as the wind suddenly gusted, bringing with it the mournful howl of the dog. "I'm not staying out here," she told Grandfather. He didn't need any urging. With Jas guiding, the two hustled up the steps and into the trailer.

The smell of mold and rotten food hit her like a pie in the face. To the right, in the kitchen area, dishes were piled in the sink. An open milk carton and a half-eaten TV dinner sat on a card table. The light was on, and fat black flies buzzed from sink to table in a frenzy.

"Whew." Jas pinched her nose. "This makes our kitchen look like an ad in *Better Homes and Gardens.*" Then she noticed the cupboard doors flung open and the pots and pans scattered on the floor. This was beyond messy. It was as if someone had been hunting for something.

She turned Grandfather in the direction of the living area. It contained a flat-screen TV and a worn recliner. Beer cans littered the floor. A dirty dog bed with a rawhide chew sat at the foot of the chair. A stack of magazines had been knocked over, and DVDs were strewn across the stained rug.

Jas gripped Grandfather's arm tightly. "Someone searched the place. Ms. Baylor?" she called, keeping her voice low. A light turned on in the hallway, and the investigator walked into the living room. Her face was pale under her bright yellow bangs. Instead of her gun, a cell phone was in her hand.

"Where's 'ooney?" Grandfather barked nervously. Jas could feel him shaking.

"He's here. Dead."

"Dead?" Jas's skin turned cold. Grandfather's arm jerked as if he'd been punched. "He's sprawled on his bedroom floor. Someone bashed his head in."

"*Hugh,*" Jas gasped.

Seventeen

❖ ❖ ❖

"THERE'S NO PROOF IT WAS HUGH." MS. BAYLOR began punching 911 on her cell phone.

"No!" Jas flew over and snatched it from her hand. "Don't call the police yet."

"I have to. It's the law."

"Not until we look around." Looney might be silent, but Jas wasn't. "The place is trashed. Hugh had to have been hunting for something. What if Looney had evidence we need? Evidence that could tie Hugh to Whirlwind? Or tell us where he took her?"

"Honey, Looney *was* the evidence. That's why he was killed. The murderer made sure he wouldn't talk."

"Murderer? It was Hugh."

"Regardless, I've got to call the police." She held out her hand.

Reluctantly, Jas gave her the phone, but

she wasn't giving up. "When the police get here, they'll seal this place off. If there is evidence that could lead us to Whirlwind, we'll never find it. Just give me a few minutes to look around," she pleaded.

Ms. Baylor opened her cell but then hesitated. "I agree: Tommy may have been smart enough to keep a record of his hauling work. But where in this trash heap would he have kept it?" Slowly, she walked into the living area, examining the mess. "It does look like Tommy knew his killer. There's no sign of forced entry. No defense wounds. And Looney did say something odd the other night after a dozen beers loosened his tongue."

"What?" Jas held her breath.

" 'Sometimes us poor folk can get the better of the rich.' We'd been talking about being 'dirt poor,' as he put it. However . . ."

"He could have been talking about information he saved to bribe a wealthy client!" Jas exclaimed.

Grandfather had sunk into the recliner. "'ooney was no dummy. I bet he 'ept some kind of record, too."

"But what kind of record? And did Hugh

find it?" Bending, Ms. Baylor scrutinized the paneled walls. "No sign of a computer hookup. He could have had a laptop—and Hugh snatched it and ran. Looney's body isn't stiff, and the blood is only partially dried. He hasn't been dead long."

"Or we could have scared him off before he found the evidence," Jas said, glad Ms. Baylor was referring to the killer as *Hugh*.

"No. Looney's been dead longer than that. And no car passed us." One ruby nail tapping her lower lip, the investigator strolled into the kitchen. Jas followed her. They stopped in front of the refrigerator. "Look, I don't dare search the freezer, cereal boxes, or loose floorboards. If the police find out I was snooping at a crime scene, they'll yank my investigator's license. But that doesn't mean you two can't."

Jas's eyes lighted. She reached for the refrigerator handle.

Ms. Baylor held up her palm like a stop sign. "Gloves, please. I've got disposable ones in my purse. Just remember—I can't wait too long to call. The bartender knows what time we left Big Mama's."

Grandfather heaved himself out of the

chair. "I'll 'art in the bedroom. 'ou stay out of 'ere, Jas."

That was fine with her. She had no desire to see Looney's bloodied head. She followed Ms. Baylor to the car. "Even when you call the police, we're on the outskirts of the county, so it will take them a while to get here."

"I know. Still, we have about fifteen, twenty minutes at the most." The investigator reached through the rolled down window and pulled out her purse. In seconds, she found latex gloves and a penlight. Rummaging a second time, she drew out a larger flashlight. "I'm going to poke around by the truck and van. Now go." She handed Jas the gloves and penlight. "You haven't much time."

Jas leaped back up the steps and into the trailer. She found Grandfather in the narrow bedroom doorway at the end of the hall. His face was gray. Raising his cane, he touched the tip to her chest, keeping her back. "I don't want 'ou to see this."

Jas swallowed hard as she helped him pull on the gloves. The metallic smell of blood wafted from the room. She didn't want to see it, either. She had nothing against Tommy

Looney, and she was sorry he'd died because of Hugh.

"We need to find something, Grandfather," she whispered. "Something that will tie Hugh to Looney's murder. Something that will help us find Whirlwind."

"'es. I'll check the 'athroom, too."

"Will you be okay?"

He inhaled deeply, "'es." Turning, he limped into the bedroom.

As Jas hurried to the kitchen, she slipped on the gloves. There wasn't much time.

Pretend you're Tommy Looney. Where would you hide something? Jas wasn't even sure what she was looking for.

Hastily, she poked through the freezer and refrigerator, checking inside opened containers. She felt the floor for loose tiles, the walls for loose panels, the bottom cupboards for false bottoms or sides. She peered under the table and chair, thinking something could have been taped to the bottoms. Under the sink, she looked inside the few boxes and jars of cleaning supplies. Then she double-checked the cupboards. Last, she opened the oven, crusty with burnt food.

Nothing. She made sure she replaced everything to its original place. Then, jumping to her feet, she started on the living room. Using the penlight, she hunted under the recliner and around and under the TV and stand. There were no curtains or shades, and the rug seemed glued to the floor. Walking the perimeter, she tapped on walls. Frustration nagged her. Maybe they were wrong, and the only record Tommy had kept was in his head. That's why Hugh had killed him.

Jas's gaze fell on the magazines. *Field and Stream. The Rifleman.* Sitting cross-legged on the floor, she leafed through every one.

Ms. Baylor stuck her head inside the trailer. "Get your grandfather outside and in the car. I told the police we stopped in to visit, found Tommy dead, and called immediately. They'll be here in ten minutes."

We need more time! But Jas didn't dare protest. She hurried to the bathroom. Grandfather was slumped tiredly on the closed toilet seat. His face was etched with sadness. Jas had forgotten that he'd known Tommy. "I'm sorry," she whispered.

He shook his head. "I didn't 'ind anything."

"That's okay." She tried to sound upbeat. "Maybe the police will find something. This was murder. They'll be thorough." *And it will take them forever.*

By the time Jas got him in the car, sirens blared in the distance. The hound dog began barking furiously.

A wild idea hit her. "I've got to check one more place," she told Ms. Baylor. "I'll meet you by the mailbox."

"Wait. Where are you—"

But headlights were turning into the drive. Jas took off clockwise around the trailer. It was a moonless night and so dark she ran right into a metal object and pitched into the grass. A wet tongue splatted her cheek along with snuffles and whines of delight. Jas threw her arms over her face, trying to protect herself from the slobbery greeting.

"Shhhh. It's all right, Digger." She patted the hound, then pushed him off her. A chain rattled as he hopped back and forth, wanting to play. "Good boy. Sit." Miraculously, he did.

Light from the trailer dimly illuminated the wooden doghouse. The hound had worn an oval in the grass. Beyond the grass were thick woods.

Jas crept to the doghouse, Digger on her heels. Clicking on the penlight, she crawled all the way around it. It was set on bricks to keep the floor dry. She shined the beam underneath but didn't see anything out of place. Then she stuck her head through the arched hole, grimacing at the odor. Twisting, she checked the sides and corners. The thin beam found a cruddy bone sticking from the straw bedding, but no records.

A lump of disappointment rose in her throat. Before pulling her head out, she aimed the light upward. The lump stuck in her chest. There, taped to the roof, was an ordinary white envelope.

Fingers trembling, she began peeling the tape. Faint voices came from the front of the trailer. She had no idea how long the police would interview Ms. Baylor and Grandfather. She had no idea how much the investigator would tell them. The insurance company needed the cooperation of the police, so obviously she would tell the truth. But that truth didn't include what Jas might find in the envelope.

Digger let out a woof, then shoved his head

inside. Jas pulled off the last of the tape. She slid the envelope underneath her T-shirt, tucking it into the waistband of her jeans.

"Good boy." She ruffled the hound's floppy ears. "Now let me out." As she crawled backward, her foot hit a food pan, making a clattering noise. She froze. Beams of light bobbed wildly to her left, and the voices grew louder. The police were following her path around the back of the trailer.

Scrambling to her feet, she bolted for the woods. Digger bounded after her. He hit the end of the chain. It snapped him to a hard stop, and he whined pitifully. "Dang you, dog." Running back, she unsnapped the chain, worried he'd hurt himself.

Together they raced into the woods.

Sticks snapped, branches slapped. Digger trotted ahead as if on a path, so Jas kept behind him. But she knew he'd head to a coon tree or a rabbit hole. She had to get back to the road or she'd be lost forever.

When she was far enough to be safely out of sight, she knelt in the leaves. The flashlight beams bounced off the trailer. They aimed at the windows, not the doghouse or the woods.

The police weren't searching for her. They were checking the perimeter. That meant they didn't realize that an idiotic teenager, pretending to be Nancy Drew, was on the loose.

Placing one palm on the envelope, Jas stood. Carefully, she made her way through the woods, keeping the trailer lights in sight. She didn't dare turn on the penlight for fear of being spotted.

What seemed like forever, she stumbled from the woods onto the road. The mailbox was twenty feet to her right. She jogged toward it, crouching behind the huge tires. Briars had scratched her arms, and branches had left knots on her forehead. Her throat was parched. But when she crinkled the envelope, a smile stretched her cheeks.

She crouched there until headlights came from the direction of the trailer. Jas hunkered lower as a car slowed at the end of the drive and then turned left. The Ford crawled past. "Jas!" Ms. Baylor hissed out the rolled down window.

She sprang from behind the tires. Yanking open the door, she piled into the backseat the same time the hound vaulted into the car. His tongue swatted her face like a wet washcloth. Jas slammed shut the door. "Go!"

"What in the world?" From the front seat, Ms. Baylor and Grandfather stared at Digger, then at Jas. She elbowed the hound off her lap. "Just *go*!"

Tires scrabbling at the gravel, the Escort rumbled down the road. "Sorry it took so long." Ms. Baylor said when they were a safe distance from Looney's. "The police asked a million questions." The investigator stared at Jas in the rearview mirror. "Well? Did you find anything?"

"An envelope taped to the top of the dog-house." She pulled it from under her T-shirt.

The Ford jerked to a stop. Ms. Baylor swung around in her seat. "What's in it?"

Jas stared at the envelope. In her adrenaline rush, she'd imagined it contained the location where Tommy had taken Whirlwind. Now she realized it could be anything—like the warranty for the doghouse or Digger's immunizations.

Fingers trembling, she opened the envelope. It contained a folded piece of notebook paper, like the kind she used at school. Slowly, she unfolded it. It was a handwritten list with dates and abbreviations. At first nothing made sense except the dates. Then Jas studied it closer, and her pulse began to race. "I think I found it. I think I found a record of the horses Tommy hauled!"

Eighteen

❧ ❧ ❧

MS. BAYLOR PUT THE CAR IN PARK AND TURNED in the seat. Her penciled eyebrows rose up to touch her bangs. "Are you certain it's Looney's records?"

"No, not certain." Leaning forward, Jas clicked on the penlight and held the sheet so Grandfather and the investigator could see it. "Look. The left-hand column contains dates. The middle contains abbreviations, maybe for places? Followed by an amount—see there's the word *one*. And the last column is . . . I don't know." She blew out a breath of frustration, suddenly realizing her initial reaction was hasty. If the list was about hauling horses, it made no sense.

"Wait, wait." Ms. Baylor studied the sheet. "I think you're right." She ran her pointy nail down to an entry dated 6/1. "That must mean

June first. Isn't that the date Whirlwind was hauled from the farm?"

Jas nodded, her excitement returning. "And look. Next to the date is HMF—High Meadows Farm! Then 'one'—one horse? And 'one hundred thirty m.'"

"One hundred and thirty miles," Ms. Baylor guessed.

"Yes, yes! One horse was hauled a hundred thirty miles from High Meadows Farm on June first. That has to be Whirlwind!" Jas began to bounce on the edge of the car seat like a little kid.

The investigator frowned. "Except the entry ends with the word *black*."

"And 'irlwind is chestnut," Grandfather said.

Jas inhaled sharply. Her fingers gripped the notebook paper. "No, that can't be right," she whispered.

Grandfather patted her hand.

"Even if it was Whirlwind, the entries don't tell us exactly where he took her," Ms. Baylor said. "It must have been his record of mileage—maybe for payment—so we could check towns in a hundred-thirty-mile radius."

"Which will give us how many towns? A hundred?" Her voice rose as she realized the futility. "It might as well be a *million*."

"I'm sorry, Jas."

She nodded. A tear trickled down her cheek. Digger stuck his nose in her face and slurped it away.

"The good news is, the police are taking Tommy's death seriously," Ms. Baylor went on. "Meaning they aren't labeling it 'drug deal gone bad' or 'neighbor shot over barking dog.' I told them about the possible link between Hugh and Tommy. Maybe something will come of it."

Jas threw herself back against the seat. "Sure. Like Hugh will convince his golfing buddy—who just happens to be the prosecutor—that Tommy bashed himself in the head."

"Come on, don't give up. I'm still looking at the horse dealers that Hugh might have worked with. Perhaps I can link one with a town a hundred thirty miles from here. Okay?" She again started the car down the road.

The hound dropped his head in Jas's lap. She stroked his soft ears, trying to hold back the despair. Every lead, every clue, every possibility seemed to turn to nothing. The information to Whirlwind's whereabouts had died with Tommy Looney. *Just as Hugh wanted.*

Jas was about to angrily scrunch the list into a ball when she decided to look at it again. Ms. Baylor was right. She couldn't let Hugh win this easily. Examining the sheet, she tried to make sense of the entries. Obviously, Tommy had hauled a horse on June 1. And HMF had to be High Meadows Farm. And hadn't he all but admitted the day she'd called him on the phone that it was a *chestnut* horse? Then why the notation "black" in the right-hand column?

She scanned the right-hand column of the other entries. Several others had "black" listed. Yet most of the other entries had names: Smith, Woodward, Gentry.

Suddenly Jas understood: "black" was not a color. It was a name. Scott Black the horse dealer! Words tumbling from her mouth, she explained her discovery to Ms. Baylor. Grandfather had fallen asleep, his head tipped forward. "And his barn's in Lexington—that's about sixty-five miles away—a hundred thirty round trip!"

"Hey, girl, you're good!" Reaching back, Ms. Baylor slapped palms with her.

"Except I thought you said Scott Black was squeaky-clean," Jas said.

"I originally thought he ran a reputable operation. But since I've been poking around, I've discovered that he's brokered a few shady deals. Which is good for my investigation—I'll have leverage when I talk with Mr. Black."

"Let's go to his house right now," Jas urged. "You've got a gun. And I'm mad enough to use it."

"Slow down, pardner." Ms. Baylor stopped the car at the intersection. "Let me handle Scott Black. If he is the agent who set up Whirlwind's sale, he'll know where she is."

"Yes!" Jas practically screamed the word. "That's why I want to talk to him *now.*"

"Only we don't want to scare him off. And"—she gave Jas a hard look—"we don't want to tip Hugh off that we know about Black."

The blood rushed from Jas's head, making her dizzy. "Oh, no. Do you think he found out we—you—were talking to Tommy? Is that why he killed him?"

Ms. Baylor shrugged one shoulder. "It's possible. Or Looney may have contacted Hugh hoping to blackmail him. Or Hugh could have been covering his tracks—getting rid of any telltale evidence. I'm sure his lawyers told him that the insurance company is proceeding with the case. Hugh's smart enough to figure out we're looking for Whirlwind."

Jas wrapped her fingers around the hound's collar. "You don't think he'd hurt her, do you?"

Ms. Baylor turned the Escort left, heading back to Second Chance Farm. The investigator's eyes darted to the rearview mirror, where they met Jas's in the glass. "Let's hope not," she said.

More waiting. Jas hated it. It had been two days since they'd found Tommy Looney. Two days since they'd discovered the information about Scott Black. Two more days of waiting to find Whirlwind.

Ms. Baylor had told Jas to pack a carry-on suitcase and keep it handy. She was confident that Scott Black would lead them to Whirlwind. Jas wanted to be as confident as the investigator. But after all this time and all the setbacks, she was too afraid.

What if they were wrong about the entries? What if Scott Black didn't know anything?

What if he refused to tell? What if Hugh bashed his head in, too?

For two days, those questions had kept Jas tossing and turning at night. Adding to her anxiety was Grandfather's refusal to take his medications for blood pressure and cholesterol. Neither she nor Mrs. Quincey were able to convince him. "Dang drugs'll kill you before a 'eart attack" was his reasoning. "Your stubbornness will kill you first," Jas had retorted. So much for acting like an adult.

"Hey, Jas, can you hold the board a little steadier?"

She glanced up. Chase stood beside her, a hammer in his hand. They'd been nailing boards to fence posts. Rand and Mr. McClain, Chase's dad, were setting posts. Grandfather was handing out nails and using the level to make sure boards and posts were straight and even. Jas had slathered him with sunscreen, made him wear a straw hat, and dragged a lawn chair from the office. Still, she couldn't stop thinking he might keel over any minute.

They'd been working all morning. Now it was noon, and the summer sun beat from a cloudless sky. Chase had taken off his T-shirt.

Sweat gleamed on his chest, trickling down his torso and into his waistband.

Jas forced her gaze from him to the board she was holding. "Sorry. I was thinking."

"About me?" Chase asked as he expertly hammered a nail.

"No. Though I do think about you," she said quickly.

He gave the nail head one last shot. "You just think more about Whirlwind."

She couldn't tell if he was serious or teasing. "Well, right now I do. That's because she's missing and you're not."

Without looking at her, he handed her the hammer and picked up another board. "What happens if you don't find her? What happens if she's missing forever?"

"Don't say that. Just hold the dang board in place." Gripping the nail, Jas hit it hard, furious at the thought of never finding Whirlwind. Her eyes blurred with tears of anger, and she bent the nail and whacked her thumb. "Shoot!" She jerked her hand back and the nail dropped into the weeds.

"Are you all right?" He set the board on the ground.

"No." Her thumb throbbed and her wrist ached from hammering all morning. "I can't believe you said that. About not ever finding Whirlwind. That's so cruel."

He studied her with his clear blue eyes. "I guess I just wanted to know what would happen to us if you never found her. The past two days you've barely spoken to me."

"Us?" she snapped. "How can I think about us now? Hugh killed some guy because he doesn't want me to find Whirlwind. And according to your father, the county police have no leads or solid evidence. That's all I can think about. Besides, it's not like we're going steady."

"No. I thought it was more than that. Guess I was wrong." With a hurt look, he yanked his T-shirt off the post. "I'm going to get lunch."

"Chase," Jas called as he strode off. But he didn't look back. Still furious—at herself—she threw down the hammer. It hit the toe of her shoe, bouncing off.

"Jas, we're breaking for lunch," Rand said as he jumped off the tractor. She picked up the bent nail and then looked around for Grandfather. He was slumped awkwardly in the lawn chair, his face bright red. Her heart flipped. "Grandfather!" she called as she dashed over.

"I'm all 'ight," he said, so softly she could barely hear.

"I need help!" she hollered. Rand and Mr. McClain hurried over. Chase's dad took Grandfather's pulse. Rand drenched a handkerchief with water from his thermos and placed it on his forehead. Grandfather tried to bat their hands away.

"He's okay," Mr. McClain said. "Heat got to him." Chase's father was a stockier version of his son. *And just as sweet,* Jas thought with a pang, wishing she hadn't snapped at Chase. But her nerves were shot; right now she had nothing more to give to a relationship.

"You've got to take it easy, old man. You're not twenty anymore," Rand jokingly told Grandfather, who scowled and retorted, "Neither are 'ou."

Everybody laughed. Jas tried to help Grandfather up, but he pulled his arm from her grasp. She knew he was embarrassed and angry. He'd worked like a bull his whole life. Now he was reduced to holding nails.

"I wonder what's for lunch," Mr. McClain said.

"Whatever we can find in Miss Hahn's refrigerator." Jas thought about their own empty refrigerator. Last night, she'd meant to ask Mrs. Quincey to take them to the grocery store. Stocking up on food: one more responsibility she was failing.

Since they'd used Rand's pickup truck to haul boards, it was parked in the pasture where they were working. "How 'bout I treat," Rand drawled as he took off his tool belt. "Burger King's not far down the road."

"Sounds great." Jas opened the passenger side door. She tried to help Grandfather climb in, but he warned her away with a growl. "We need to pick up Chase," she said to Rand.

"Nope. The kid eats too much." Rand winked at Jas. "Oh, wait. I've got coupons."

She rode in the bed of the truck, bouncing as it wound up the side of the hill. They caught up with Chase by the gate in the fence that enclosed the barn area. "Get in, boy," Rand called out his open window.

"Thanks. I'll walk." He opened the gate for them.

"We're getting fast food," his father said. He was squashed between Rand and Grandfather in the front seat.

Chase shifted his eyes toward Jas, then quickly looked away. "Nah."

"Come on," Jas urged as the truck rumbled through the opening. "You know you're dying for a bacon cheeseburger, dripping with grease, and a giant order of fries." She could almost see him salivate.

"All right." Reluctantly, he gave in. He shut the gate and, tossing his shirt into the truck bed, vaulted over the tailgate. But he settled against the tire wheel, as far from her as he could.

Sorry. I was an idiot. Jas rehearsed an apology. Hopefully he'd talk to her at some point on the way to Burger King. Maybe if she explained why she'd freaked, he'd understand. However, sooner or later, if she kept acting like a brat, he would quit understanding.

The truck drove slowly past the barn and office, scattering geese, chickens, and dogs. Tilly barked at the wheels. Digger was in quarantine, baying his displeasure at being locked up. Monster and Hope ran behind the truck. Since Monster had gotten out of quarantine, the two dogs were inseparable.

Like Chase and I used to be. Jas watched him from the corner of her eye. His gaze was riveted on the roof of the truck cab. She was about to say something when Rand braked in front of the gate that led to the driveway.

Chase jumped out. Jas followed, shooing animals out of the way so the truck could pass through. When he shut the gate, he was careful not to meet her eyes.

A horn beeped. A cherry-red convertible was driving up from the main road. Lucy waved from the driver's seat. "Hey y'all! Come see my new car!"

"Wow," Chase murmured. "What a sweet Mustang."

Instantly, the guys spilled from the truck, even Grandfather. Jas could have cared less. Except that Chase was fawning over the car *and* Lucy. Jas scowled, kicked gravel, and patted Reese, who hopped over on his three legs with a tennis ball. She tossed the ball across the lawn. Then, figuring she'd rather be a good sport than a jealous witch, she sauntered over. By then, the hood was up and all four guys were bent over, inspecting the engine. "Nice car, Lucy," she said, trying to sound as if she meant it.

The older girl was fluffing her hair, her gaze aimed in the sideview mirror. "It is, isn't it."

Jas slid one finger along the shiny chrome. "A present?"

"Kind of." She pulled lip gloss from a teeny purse.

"From your dad?"

"What's with the interrogation?" Lucy shot her an annoyed look as she slid gloss over her pursed lips.

Jas frowned, wondering why Lucy was avoiding her questions. Chase was right—it was ludicrous to think that Lucy was behind the leaks to Hugh. Yet, how else could she afford an expensive car? It certainly wasn't the money she made riding horses for Mrs. Vandevender. And Lucy's mom was a single parent who worked in a doctor's office. There was a dad, but he lived in Richmond, and according to Lucy, he was a "jerk who married some twenty-year-old." Had Lucy made a deal with a devil named Hugh?

"Excuse me." Lucy opened the car door so fast that Jas had to jump out of the way. "How do you like her, guys?" she asked as she waltzed toward the front of the car.

Whistles and comments of praise rang from under the hood. "What do you say, Pop?" Chase whacked his dad affectionately on the shoulder. "I'll have my learner's in a month."

"Sorry. It's your mother's old Honda for you," Mr. McClain said, and Chase groaned.

Jas headed back to the truck, her thoughts still on Lucy. Devious spy or not, she didn't trust the girl. Or any of the volunteers, really. Mr. Muggins was always hanging around. And George and Rand asked too many questions. The only people she trusted were Miss Hahn, Grandfather, and Chase—who wasn't talking to her, anyway.

"Jas!" Miss Hahn flagged her down from the kitchen doorway. "Phone call for you."

"Can you take a message? We're headed to lunch." *If Lucy would ever move her stupid car.*

"You're welcome to come, Diane," Rand offered as he closed the hood of the Mustang.

"Yes to lunch, no to a message," Miss Hahn said. "It's Ms. Baylor, Jas."

"It is?" Jas broke into a run. "Don't wait for me," she hollered over her shoulder as she crossed the lawn, Reese bounding beside her, still wanting to play.

"You sure?" Rand hollered.

"Positive!" The conversation with the investigator was too important to rush through. Jas raced past Miss Hahn. Flinging open the kitchen door, she flew inside and picked up the phone. "Hi, Ms. Baylor."

"Jas, I've got exciting news. Pack your bags—you're going to Florida. I've found Whirlwind!"

Nineteen

❧ ❧ ❧

JAS BURST INTO TEARS. SOBBING, SHE REACHED for a box of tissues, pulled one out, and tried to staunch the flow. "I'm sooo . . ." She struggled, unable to speak. Finally, the sobs receded and she was able to ask, "Is Whirlwind all right?"

"She's fine. Beautiful. I'll tell you all about her when I pick you up at the airport."

"You're in Florida already?"

"Hey, when I get a solid lead, I work fast. Now, grab a pencil and paper. I've booked you a flight to Gainesville. You leave early tomorrow morning."

Jas's head was whirling, but she quickly wrote down the information, double-checking every detail.

"If Miss Hahn can't take you to the airport, call this limo service." Ms. Baylor gave her a phone number. "The insurance company will pay for it."

"Got it. Got everything." Jas's fingers tightened on the phone receiver. "Ms. Baylor, are you . . . are you sure it's Whirlwind?" She was afraid to ask but needed to know. She couldn't stand any more disappointments.

"Ninety-five percent. She matches the photo, I found the scar, and her circumstances are right. Your identification will make it one hundred percent."

"Scott Black told you where to find her?"

"Honey, no more discussion over the phone. And you keep this strictly between you and Miss Hahn, you hear?"

"Yes." Jas lowered her voice, understanding what Ms. Baylor was saying. *No more leaked information.* "I'll see you tomorrow afternoon."

"Don't sound so distressed. Just think— one more day." She could hear the glee in Ms. Baylor's voice. "One more day before you see your horse."

That night, Jas went out to the pasture to say goodbye to Shadow. Climbing over the fence, she saw him at the bottom of the hill grazing with the other horses. As soon as he saw her, he raised his head and nickered.

She sat on the top board, whistled, and held out a carrot. His ears pricked and he broke into a canter. "Hey, easy. Whoa!" she gasped as he charged toward her, worried he'd jump over the fence—or over her.

But he slid to a halt and plopped his muzzle in her lap, almost knocking her off the fence. Laughing, she grabbed his mane to keep from falling.

"Such terrible manners," she scolded when he snatched the carrot from her hand. "I came to tell you goodbye. I'll be away for a day or two. When I come back, I might have a friend for you. Her name's Whirlwind." Just saying the mare's name made her heart thump. Was it really going to happen?

She tried to remember the last time she'd seen Whirlwind. It was the afternoon of the day before she'd found the dead mare in the paddock. She'd schooled Whirlwind over a course of fences, getting ready for an upcoming show. The mare had been perfect—smooth, steady, and graceful. Hugh had been so delighted, he'd told Jas to cool her off and put her away after one round.

Instead, Jas had unsaddled her. Then, jumping on her bareback, she'd ridden her behind the barn and down a path into the shadowy woods. Hugh would never know, she told herself after every secret jaunt that spring. He was too busy calling clients and making deals.

Not that they galloped recklessly through the trees. No, the two walked to a stream. Whirlwind would duck her head, drink, then paw with her hoof, splashing water. Jas would lie on the mare's neck, arms dangling, dreaming of a horse of her own. Not just any horse. *Whirlwind.*

Shadow bumped her arm, wanting more. "Sorry, Mr. Greedy, no more carrots." She scratched under his forelock. His coat felt sticky in the humid evening, and flies buzzed around her head. "Now, when Whirlwind comes, I want you to be nice to her. No biting and being bossy. Okay?" He tossed his head as if agreeing. "Nicer than I've been to Chase," she added, glancing over her shoulder.

The barn and office were dark. Chase and his father had returned to the farm after lunch but had immediately left. She'd tried to call him to say goodbye and to tell him the exciting news, but he didn't pick up his cell phone, and no one was home.

Or he was avoiding her.

Not that she blamed him. She'd been such a pain. Still, he'd worked as hard as she had to find Whirlwind, and he deserved to hear the good news—despite Ms. Baylor's warning.

Sighing, she gave Shadow a last pat goodbye. Jumping off the fence, she watched as he trotted back to the other horses. She'd try Chase later. In fact, she'd call until he answered, even if it took all night. After all, it wasn't as if she'd be able to sleep. She was way too excited.

"Your grandfather will be in good hands," Miss Hahn reassured Jas as they drove to the Charlottesville Airport early in the morning. "Mrs. Quincey cared for her husband for many years."

Before she killed him with rum cake.

"I'll check on him every morning and evening," she went on. "And he'll be helping Rand during the day."

"Remind Rand to make sure Grandfather wears his hat and sunscreen," Jas said. "And drinks plenty of water—he can't get overheated. And he needs his nap after lunch."

"I will. Try not to worry. Concentrate on Whirlwind. Now, as for the farm business, I've good news." Miss Hahn began to talk about the donations that were coming in. "We're not out of the woods yet, but because of the brochures you kids sent out, donations are up."

"Thank goodness." Jas was glad to see a smile back on Miss Hahn's face.

"Just in time, too. That dog Monster eats as much as a horse," she grumbled, *affectionately,* Jas noticed. "And don't get me started on Digger. He's true to his name. There are four holes in the quarantine stall. But I think Daryl James, the farmer down the road, will adopt him. He's got coonhounds galore, yet loves each one like a child."

As Jas listened, she stared out the window at the orange glow of the sun rising over the giant box stores and car dealerships on Route 29. She'd never flown before, but Miss Hahn was going inside the terminal with her. Plus, she had prepped her carefully on dos and don'ts, especially for when she had to switch planes in Atlanta.

She hadn't told Grandfather the reason she was going to Florida—too afraid that he would blurt it to Mrs. Quincey or another volunteer. Miss Hahn had made up a story about Jas needing to be in Florida for an emergency visit with her mother, Iris. Which was a laugh. Iris was working at some racetrack in Florida, but Jas hadn't heard from her since last year's Christmas card. Still, on short notice, the lie had to do.

Even worse, Jas had never talked to Chase. Finally, after midnight, she'd left a message on his cell phone. *I can't tell you everything,* she'd told him, *even though I promised no more secrets.* She had told him that Ms. Baylor had found Whirlwind but not where. And she'd said she was sorry.

Would Chase forgive her for just leaving? For not telling him the details? The thought that he might not made her ache. At the same time, she was brimming with joy. *Whirlwind.* If Ms. Baylor was right, she would soon be with her beloved horse.

"We're here," Miss Hahn said.

Jas grabbed her carry-on bag from the backseat. Half an hour later, she had her ticket and was ready to go through security. "Thank you." She hugged Miss Hahn, and for a minute, they kept their arms wrapped around each other. Then Jas pulled away. "I'll call you as soon as I know something."

"No, you call as soon as you arrive in Gainesville." Worry shimmered in Miss Hahn's brown eyes. "You realize I trust Ms. Baylor; otherwise I'd never let you do this alone."

"I *am* almost fourteen," Jas reminded her, trying to sound confident, although inside she was a bundle of nerves. Ms. Baylor was ninety-five percent sure the mare was Whirlwind. That left five percent of doubt. And suddenly, that doubt seemed huge.

"I know. Now pay attention," Miss Hahn added in her no-nonsense tone. "Watch the flight numbers and times, and don't forget your bag when you disembark."

"Gotcha." Jas smiled a goodbye and then stepped into the security line. Waving one last time, Miss Hahn disappeared out the front doors.

The line snaked slowly toward the security checkpoint. Jas clutched her ticket in one hand, her bag in the other. Even though she was surrounded by people, she felt terribly alone. She missed Grandfather. She missed Chase. If she had a cell phone, she would have called him to say goodbye. He'd be half asleep and sweetly goofy.

But she didn't have a phone. The message would have to do until she returned.

Six hours later, Jas landed in Gainesville. It

was three o'clock in the afternoon. When she stepped from the plane, the humidity enveloped her. The sun was hidden under clouds, and puddles dotted the tarmac as if it had recently rained. Before landing, the captain of the plane had mentioned a tropical storm. But the speaker system was so garbled, she hadn't understood his exact words. Still, even without the sun shining, Jas broke into a sweat. Ms. Baylor had forgotten to mention the gosh-awful heat.

Her carry-on banging against her leg, she followed the other passengers into the small terminal. She glanced around, looking for Ms. Baylor's daisy yellow hair. The investigator had promised to meet her, but the flight had arrived early.

Jas waited just inside the entrance in the air-conditioning. Streams of cars drove past the double glass doors. Some discharged passengers; others picked them up. Jas checked the watch she'd borrowed from Miss Hahn. Ms. Baylor was ten minutes late. Hunger pangs hit her. She'd rushed to make her connecting flight in Atlanta, so she hadn't had time to grab lunch. And, really, she'd been too nervous to eat.

Jas shivered despite the feeble air-conditioning. Outside, a car slowed along the curb, and her hopes picked up. But it was a man in the driver's seat. A man who leaned over to stare out the passenger window at her.

She gasped. *Hugh.*

Jas dove through the double doors. The man straightened and the car drove off. She noted bumper stickers that read *Universal Studios* and *My Son Is an Honor Student at Gainesville Elementary.*

Not Hugh. Some Gainesville father. She rubbed her forehead, tired. Her nightmares about Whirlwind were making her loopy. There was no way Hugh could have found out she was in Gainesville. She'd been too careful.

"Welcome to Florida, Jas."

She turned. A woman with honey-brown hair wearing big sunglasses and a floral dress with spaghetti straps came out of the terminal doors. "Ms. Baylor?" Jas asked, recognizing the investigator by the purse slung over her shoulder.

"Sorry I'm late. I've been hunting for you inside. We must have missed each other." She slid her glasses to the top of her head. "Are you all right?"

"Hungry. And tired. I slept about an hour last night. Too excited."

"I couldn't sleep, either."

"And I barely recognized you," Jas admitted sheepishly. "For some reason I was expecting Shasta."

Ms. Baylor laughed. "I left that gal at Big Mama's. Come on. Let's get you something to eat."

"A drive-through, please. I can't wait another minute to see Whirlwind."

Twenty minutes later, they were speeding through Gainesville. Jas ate a chicken sandwich while Ms. Baylor filled her in. "Whirlwind is stabled at a top show barn outside of town. Her owner, a Mrs. Pavia, bought her from Scott Black. The transaction was aboveboard, and Mrs. Pavia believes she owns a Thoroughbred mare named Early Star."

Early Star. A picture of the dead horse in the paddock popped into Jas's head. Had Hugh killed the real Early Star in his greed? Had the mare once been some girl's show horse? Or had she raced on the track, trying her hardest, never suspecting she'd end up . . .

"How does Whirlwind look?" Jas asked quickly, trying to chase away the gloomy thoughts. "Is she healthy? Happy?"

"She's had excellent care. Gerald Fordham, the trainer at the barn, knows his stuff. I visited him this morning. Mr. Fordham has been cooperative."

Finishing her sandwich, Jas started on the fries. As she ate, she peered out the side window. It was only about four in the afternoon, yet the sky was dark. "The pilot said something about a storm."

"Unfortunately." Ms. Baylor sounded so uncharacteristically anxious that Jas turned to look at her. Leaning forward, the investigator flicked on the car's radio. "They've been broadcasting hurricane warnings."

"I thought the pilot said a tropical storm warning," Jas said.

"Well, this *is* hurricane season and we are in Florida. It seems Hurricane Hilda has taken an abrupt left turn. Forecasts range from the storm missing this area completely to high winds and four inches of rain."

"Rain we could use in Virginia." Jas stuck the last fry in her mouth. "So how did you convince Scott Black to tell you where Whirlwind was?"

Ms. Baylor smiled. "I used gangsta threats sugarcoated with Southern charm. The gentleman crumbled like a pecan pie crust."

"A weather update . . ." came over the radio, and Ms. Baylor turned it up.

"Hurricane Hilda, a category two hurricane, is expected to reach the Gainesville area by eight o'clock this evening. All precautions should be . . ."

"Category two isn't too threatening," Ms. Baylor said. "And folks here are prepared."

Crumpling her fry wrapper, Jas dropped it in the bag. "I can't wait to see Whirlwind."

"Won't be much longer. But, honey, a warning. Mr. Fordham has been cooperative but Mrs. Pavia, Whirlwind's owner, has not. She'll be there when we arrive." Ms. Baylor snorted delicately. "No doubt with a lawyer or two."

Instantly, the fries felt like lead in Jas's stomach. "What can she do?"

"Not much if the horse is Whirlwind. The mare is evidence in a crime and was sold under fraudulent conditions. But she can get her lawyers to delay extradition to Virginia."

"Extradition?"

"That means surrendering a criminal to another state or location. In this case, I'm using it to mean surrendering evidence, which is Whirlwind, from Florida to Virginia."

Twisting her fingers together, Jas stared straight ahead. For some reason, she'd naively believed that once they found Whirlwind, they'd simply take her home. Except now she realized, Where was her home? Whirlwind didn't belong to Mrs. Pavia or Hugh. And she didn't belong to Jas.

"Ms. Baylor?"

"Honey, call me Marietta. I've had enough of this formal stuff. We're going to be together for a while."

"Marietta, what will happen to Whirlwind if she is extradited?"

"Right now she's property of the insurance company. So it depends on what they choose to do with her."

A great idea flashed into Jas's mind. "Can I use your phone to call Miss Hahn? I need to tell her I arrived safely. I was supposed to call as soon as I got here. More importantly, I want to ask her to call Mr. Jenkins. She needs to tell him that if— no, *when*—Whirlwind comes back to Virginia, the mare needs to stay at Second Chance Farm."

The mare would love it at the farm, Jas knew. She'd be surrounded by people who appreciated her *just because she existed*. Her days of standing in a stall 24/7 would be over.

She could roll in the dirt and graze like a real horse. Jas would groom her until she shone and would ride her in the woods. The mare would never have to trot around a ring again—unless she wanted to. And best of all, she and Whirlwind would never be apart again.

Forgetting about Hugh, the hurricane, and that five percent of doubt, Jas grinned excitedly. For the first time in months, true happiness filled her.

Twenty

❖ ❖ ❖

"YOU CAN CALL TO LET MISS HAHN KNOW you're safe." Marietta slid her cell phone from her purse. "But, Jas, you know as well as I do that Whirlwind can't stay at Second Chance Farm. It's too risky. She needs to be somewhere where Hugh can't find her."

Jas's elation deflated. Marietta was right: as long as Hugh was free, neither Whirlwind nor the farm would be safe.

"Mr. Jenkins and I already discussed it over the phone," Marietta went on. "I suggested a farm in Harrisonburg, not too far from Stanford. I personally know the owner. She loves horses as much as you do."

Jas nodded numbly. Whirlwind's safety was more important than her own wishes. Even if it meant she might not be able to see the mare until after Hugh's trial. She could live with that. She'd *have* to live with that.

Marietta punched in a number and handed her phone to Jas. When Miss Hahn answered, Jas told her that she'd arrived safely and was headed to see Whirlwind. "Any news about Tommy's murder?" she asked before disconnecting. Miss Hahn replied that there was no news. And that Grandfather was as fine and as stubborn as usual.

Jas said goodbye, then quickly added, "Tell Chase I miss him. Will you? I didn't get to tell him goodbye."

When Jas turned the phone off, Marietta glanced at her. "Nothing about Tommy's investigation?"

"No. Why haven't the police arrested Hugh? He's got to be their only suspect."

"Sweetie, if homicides were that easy to solve, the United States wouldn't be the murder capital of the world. Here we are."

Springing forward in her seat, Jas stared out the windshield. She'd been so busy talking, she hadn't realized they were now in the middle of horse country.

Unlike the Shenandoah Valley of Virginia,

central Florida was fairly flat. A long white barn with a black roof sat far off the road. A few groves of trees shaded the barn, which was surrounded by paddocks that were laid out like checkerboard squares. Each paddock had a run-in shed and automatic waterer. Jas counted about ten of them. They were fenced with white posts and boards and separated from each other by grassy aisles. Beyond the paddocks was a field bordered by a thick grove of loblolly pines and oaks. There were no horses anywhere. In the barn, Jas guessed, due to the storm warnings.

Marietta turned right at a sign that read SWEET SPRINGS STABLE. QUALITY HUNTERS AND JUMPERS. TRAINING AND LESSONS: GERALD FORDHAM ESQ. She drove the rental car up the winding driveway lined with palms. Newly paved, of course. Before they reached the parking area, they passed a huge outdoor ring filled with freshly painted jumps: oxers, in-and-outs, a brush box and brick wall.

Except for the palms, the farm could have been High Meadows' twin. In other words, it was everything that Second Chance Farm wasn't.

"Let me do the talking," Marietta said as

she parked between an Escalade and a BMW. "Mrs. Pavia believes her wealth entitles her to anything she wants." She pointed to the sportier car. "Like her M6—costs over a hundred grand."

Jas broke into a sweat. And not because of the sticky heat that rushed into the car the second she opened the door. "Please don't talk too long. I *have* to see Whirlwind!"

"Patience, darlin'. Do you have rain gear with you?" She gestured to the ceiling of thick, gray clouds. "In case the heavens open before we leave."

Jas dug in her bag for her Windbreaker. Marietta draped a rose-colored raincoat and matching umbrella over her own arm. Then she led the way to the stable office. The wind had picked up, whipping the tops of the palms. Jas noticed that storm shutters already secured the office windows.

The door opened into a tack room, which was frigid compared to outside and dark because of the shuttered windows. Light and voices spilled from an open doorway.

"Hello? Mr. Fordham?" Marietta called, and a man bustled from an office and turned on the tack room lights. He wore riding breeches and tall black boots. A woman, her cranberry-red lips pinched as if ready for war, followed behind him.

Marietta introduced everyone. "We need to make this fast," Gerald Fordham said. "I've secured the barn. However, I need to get home before the hurricane hits."

Ignoring Jas, Mrs. Pavia glared at Marietta. "This nonsense about Early Star being another horse should only take an instant to rectify." Her tone was as icy as the tack room. "I purchased the mare from a reputable dealer. I have a contract and her registration. My lawyers have assured me that the sale is legal and binding."

Jas crooked one brow. It appeared that Mrs. Pavia would be more lethal than any storm. The woman was dressed in a waist-hugging suit jacket and skirt made of linen. Nylons, open-toed pumps, and a matching purse finished the outfit. Jas wondered if she'd come from her lawyers or if this was her normal horse-wrangling outfit. More than likely, she was one of those wealthy owners who left the riding, grooming, and patting to the hired help. Jas had met too many of them at High Meadows Farm.

She stepped toward the woman. "Don't

worry, Mrs. Pavia." Jas kept her own voice steely. "It will take me only an instant to know if the horse is Whirlwind."

"Fine, then. Let's get this over with. You'll quickly see that this *Whirlwind* you're looking for is not my Star." Mrs. Pavia's high heels rapped angrily across the wooden floor of the tack room. Murmuring soothing platitudes, Gerald Fordham hurried after her.

Marietta gave Jas an encouraging smile. "Ready?"

Jas nodded. As she headed from the tack room, she clenched and unclenched her fingers. *I'm ninety-five percent sure it's Whirlwind,* she repeated Marietta's words. She had to believe them.

The huge barn was modern and well kept. A perfectly raked aisle stretched left and right from the tack room door. About twenty-five stalls opened into the aisle. Overhead fans swirled the sultry air. Electronic bug zappers zinged discreetly in the distance.

Turning right, Jas followed Marietta, Gerald, and Mrs. Pavia down the aisle. A state-of-the-art washroom; a clipping area; a restroom; and a supply room filled with balms, sprays, supplements, and totes full of brushes were located on the right side of the aisle. On the left of the aisle, the horses were housed in roomy stalls. Whirlwind had been living in four-star accommodations.

Gerald stopped in front of one of the stalls. The tops of all the doors were barred so the horses couldn't hang their heads over. "I want to introduce you to Magic Man, four-time Florida Hunter Champion."

Jas frowned, wondering why he was stalling when all she wanted to do was see Whirlwind. Then she noticed Mrs. Pavia on her cell phone, probably trying to roust a lawyer. Marietta was on her phone, too. The investigator held up one finger as if telling Jas to hold on one minute.

Impatiently, Jas peeked through the bars. Magic Man wore a fly sheet, although she hadn't seen one fly. He also wore a cribbing strap. And no wonder. The handsome Thoroughbred was probably in his stall day and night. No chance to let off energy rolling, grazing, and hanging out with his buddies. So he'd developed the horrible habit of cribbing, or wind sucking. She also noticed the stall walls were high and solid so even in the barn the horses couldn't see each other. Typical of a show barn; what wasn't typical was the piped in classical music.

"You play music for the horses?" she asked Gerald.

"Of course. That way they can't hear each other, so they think they're alone."

"But horses are herd animals," Jas said, horrified. Even Hugh hadn't gone *that* far.

"True. But if they don't see or hear each other, they never get attached or herd bound. Nothing worse than a young horse neighing for his friend when he's in the show ring."

Jas blinked in amazement. Had she been just as brainwashed when she'd lived at High Meadows?

"Where's Whirlwind?" she suddenly asked, charging past him down the aisle.

"Wait." Gerald's boots thudded behind her. Even Marietta had snapped her phone shut and was hurrying after her. Jas glanced in each stall as she passed: black, bay, too tall, too short. Abruptly, she skidded to a halt and stared through the bars of the end stall. A chestnut horse faced her, its head hanging. It was covered with a fly sheet, its mane was covered with a mane tamer, and the tail was wrapped in a tail bag.

Still, Jas recognized the fine head, the soft brown eyes, the white star.

"Whirlwind." She slammed open the latch on the stall door. *"Whirlwind!"*

At the sound of Jas's voice, Whirlwind threw up her head. Her ears flicked. Dancing forward, she greeted Jas with excited puffs and whickers.

Jas flung her arms around the mare's neck. Tears streamed down her cheeks. "I can't believe it," she whispered into the mane tamer. "I can't believe it's you!"

Jas pulled back, wanting to examine every inch of the mare. Whirlwind snuffled her wet cheek, and Jas burst into teary laughter—of joy and relief. "I can't believe I finally found you!"

"That's your proof?" she heard Mrs. Pavia protest. "As far as we know, Ms. Baylor, you hired some actress to stage this touching reunion."

"Oh? Then who coached the horse?" Marietta asked. "It's obvious that this horse and Jas know each other."

Mrs. Pavia swept into the stall. Grabbing hold of the halter, she jerked the mare away from Jas. Furious, Jas curled her fingers into fists. There was no way this woman was keeping her from her horse. She stepped forward, shaking with anger, but Marietta touched her shoulder. "Let me handle this."

"I paid two hundred fifty thousand dollars for this horse from a reputable dealer," Mrs. Pavia ranted. "There's no way I'm letting you take her."

"Caveat emptor," Marietta murmured as she pulled her BlackBerry from her purse. "Gerald, do you have pad and paper? I want to make sure that Mrs. Pavia has the phone number for Hugh Robicheaux. He's the man in Virginia who fraudulently sold Whirlwind to Scott Black, your so-called reputable dealer."

"What am I supposed to do with that information?" Mrs. Pavia demanded.

"Give it to your lawyers." Marietta aimed an unladylike look at the other woman. "Now please let go of Whirlwind."

"Oh, oh," Mrs. Pavia sputtered as she waded in her heels through the shavings, giving the investigator a wide berth. She stopped in front of the trainer. "Gerald! *Do* something."

As soon as the woman let go of the halter, Whirlwind spun toward Jas. The mare's eyes were white-rimmed with fear. Jas slipped one arm over the horse's withers, the other around her neck. "I'll never let you go, ever again," she promised.

"I'm sorry, Mrs. Pavia," a red-faced Gerald was saying. "When Ms. Baylor came yesterday, she brought quite a bit of evidence. So I was pretty sure Early Star was the horse she was looking for." Unable to hide a smile, he gestured toward Jas and Whirlwind. "Horses don't lie, so it's obvious these two belong to each other."

"You'll *all* be hearing from my lawyers." Mrs. Pavia shook her finger at Gerald and then Marietta before marching up the aisle.

"Excuse my client," Gerald said. "She does love this horse."

Love this horse? Jas snorted. "Has she ever groomed Whirlwind? Patted her? Fed her a carrot?"

Mr. Fordham seemed confused by the questions. Jas waved him away. "Never mind." Without asking permission, she began unfastening the Velcro straps of the mane tamer and then the tail wrap. As she worked, smoothing Whirlwind's coat, soothing her with soft words, she let go of her anger, her fears. She'd found Whirlwind. Let Mrs. Pavia bring an army of lawyers. Nothing was going to take her away from Jas again.

"Mrs. Pavia discovered the mare herself,

through a friend who'd used Scott Black," Gerald said as if that explained the woman's behavior. Leaning against the doorjamb, Marietta listened. Jas started on the fly sheet. Seeing Whirlwind all fancied up was too much.

"When she took me to see Early Star, I was wary because I'd never dealt with Mr. Black before," he continued. "But when I saw how fabulous the mare was, I urged Mrs. Pavia to buy her on the spot."

"Where did you see the mare?" Marietta asked.

"At a barn in Lexington. We flew to Roanoke, then drove to Lexington. Black met us at a farm—I think it was called Rolling Acres. We had the mare vanned to Florida the next day."

"No vet check?"

"We had one done here in Florida—she vetted clean. Black gave us a week's trial with the horse, which I requested. As Mrs. Pavia said, everything seemed to be in order." He shrugged. "I never suspected she wasn't the horse on the registration."

"The real Early Star was murdered," Jas said flatly.

Gerald started. "What?"

"Hugh, Whirlwind's owner, pois—"

"Jas." Marietta shot her a look of warning, then said to the trainer, "The lawyer from the insurance company is faxing documents so we can take possession of Whirlwind. A Florida judge will have to approve seizure and transport of the horse, so it may take a day or two. We want this all to be aboveboard."

"Fine." Gerald nervously checked his watch. "In the meantime, I have to leave. The horses are fed, watered, and safe here in the barn. The hurricane's supposed to hit early tonight, and my condo needs to be secured. I suggest you ladies get to a hotel as soon as possible."

"I've already made reservations at the Marriot Inn. They assured me it has weathered many a storm."

"I'm not leaving Whirlwind," Jas said.

The two stopping talking to stare at her.

"I'm sleeping here. You must have a cot for horse shows."

"Yes, we do," Gerald said. "Stashed in the supply room. You're welcome to stay. The barn is hurricane proof, but I had to turn off the motion-detecting security system. It would be going off all night because of flying branches and debris."

Marietta frowned. "Jas, I'm going with Gerald to the office to check for a fax. We'll talk about you staying here when I get back." She sounded like a disapproving parent.

"Fine." *But I won't change my mind.* Jas unbuckled the fly sheet, slid it off Whirlwind, and ran her palm over the mare's sleek coat. Laying her cheek against her shoulder, Jas sighed with happiness. Finally, she stepped back and, hands on hips, ran her gaze from the mare's ears to her tail. She wanted to drink in every inch.

Turning her head, Whirlwind looked at her, her eyes deep and brown. Jas bit her lip, trying not to cry again. It was hard to believe *this* was real.

"And no matter what Marietta says, I'm not leaving you," Jas said. "Which means I better figure out where to sleep."

Picking up the fly sheet and wraps, she walked down to the supply room. She found a cot, a pillow, flashlights, and blankets along with every type of grooming device. What she didn't find was evidence that the horses were treated as anything except commodities. There were no carrots tucked away in buckets or goofy names like Buster and Pal tacked on the stall doors. There were no paisley helmet covers or drawings of horses with stick legs and huge heads. Actually, there were no signs of kids at all. No signs of horse-crazy riders who adored their mounts no matter how furry or swaybacked.

Grabbing up a grooming tote, Jas hurried back to Whirlwind's stall. "I've *got* to get you out of this place," she said when she unlatched the door. She set down the tote and pulled out a soft brush. Not that the mare was dirty. Far from it—she was too clean. It was Jas who needed grooming "therapy." She'd found Whirlwind. The mare was fine. They were taking her back to Virginia. Still, butterflies fluttered in Jas's stomach. She couldn't shake the ominous feeling that *Hugh was out there*.

"Good news!" Marietta appeared in the doorway. "Scott Black has agreed to testify against Hugh in return for immunity."

"What does that mean exactly?" Jas stopped brushing. "Before I jump up and down with joy?"

"It means we've got Hugh. Not only will Scott Black testify that Hugh contacted him about selling a Thoroughbred named Early

Star, but he can also link Hugh to Tommy Looney, who delivered the mare to Black's farm in Lexington." Marietta's face broke into a smile of triumph. "Most importantly, Jas, it means that Hugh Robicheaux will be behind bars for a looong time."

Twenty-one

✤ ✤ ✤

"YES!" JAS AND MARIETTA CHEERED AND SLAPPED palms as if their underdog team had finally won. Jas ruffled Whirlwind's mane, scratching her favorite spot behind her ears. "Did you hear that?" she told the mare. "Hugh the horse killer is finally getting what he deserves." The mare wiggled her lips. "Look, she's as happy as we are."

"She'll be happier when we get her out of this prison." Marietta grimaced at the bars on the door. "I've been here three times now. Never once have I seen a horse out of its stall."

"You noticed, too. Creepy, huh?" Jas continued brushing. "If Hugh goes to jail, will we be able to take Whirlwind to Second Chance Farm? I want her to experience life as a real horse."

"Not right away. Our court system moves

as slow as molasses." Marietta pulled her cell phone from her purse. "Let's make sure the lawyers have an airtight case against Hugh first. Then he'll have no reason to come after Whirlwind. I'm going to take some photos with my phone and e-mail them to the lawyer's office. Can you lead her into the aisle where there's more light?"

For the next ten minutes, Jas helped Marietta photograph Whirlwind. The investigator snapped pictures of the mare's head and white stripe, her stockings, and the scar under her forelock. "These will be dated so Hugh can't claim someone took them last spring."

"Instead he can claim we painted a horse to look like Whirlwind."

Marietta arched one brow. "He can claim all he wants. I had Gerald fax his statement before he left. Hugh's arrogant, but there's no way he can accuse *all* of us of being crooks."

Just then, rat-a-tat-tats sounded on the roof of the barn. "Rain," Jas said. "You better hurry and get to the hotel, Marietta."

"Hotel? Like I'm going to let you stay here alone? Not gonna happen, honey. There's a comfortable sofa in the office. However, I will need to borrow some of those blankets you found."

"You don't have to stay here," Jas protested. "I'm perfectly capable . . ."

Marietta raised her hand. "I know you are, sweetheart. You've had to handle a lot this summer. For a kid of almost fourteen, you've done incredibly well. But quit arguing and accept the fact that I'm staying here, too." She smiled. "Hey, I don't want to leave Whirlwind, either. This lady wasn't easy to find."

"Thank you, Marietta. For finding her."

"My pleasure." Marietta snapped her phone shut. "Photos done and sent." Overhead, the tapping changed to drumming. Outside, the wind rattled the barn's high double doors at each end of the aisle. Inside, the temperature dropped. "Now let's drag out those blankets and shut off those fans. It's going to be a chilly night."

Clicking on a flashlight, Jas checked her wristwatch. Eleven o'clock. She rolled over on the cot that she'd placed in front of Whirlwind's open door. Except for one blanket beneath her, there wasn't much padding, and she couldn't get comfortable. Not that she could've slept with all the racket.

The rain pelted the roof, sounding as sharp

as hail. The wind battered the end doors, which strained at their latches. The electricity had gone out, so the closed-up barn was dark, except for two emergency lights. Yet, beneath the furious sounds of the storm, Jas heard something else: snorts, snuffles, whinnies. The horses were talking to each other.

Lacing her fingers behind her head, she listened. She remembered reading how prisoners of war, held in isolation, had communicated by knocking on the walls. It seemed as if the horses had created their own system despite all Gerald's work to keep them separated. She wondered what they were saying. Were they afraid of the storm? Did they hate being trapped alone behind barred walls? Were they sending calming and encouraging messages?

Sitting up, she aimed a flashlight into Whirlwind's stall. Instantly, the mare's ears pricked. "You're wide awake, too," Jas said when she came over. "I was too excited to sleep. Plus, I never want to take my eyes off you." Whirlwind nibbled Jas's hair, making her laugh. "Maybe a walk would help us both. We could visit the other horses. Reassure them that it will be okay."

Standing, Jas pushed the cot to the side.

Then she hooked a lead line to Whirlwind's leather halter. EARLY STAR was written on the metal name plate. Jas wished she could get rid of the halter, but she hadn't thought to bring one to replace it.

Whirlwind eagerly strode into the aisle. They walked up and down, stretching their legs. Lightning flashed through a row of skylights overhead, illuminating a path. Jas tried to tune out the sounds of the hurricane. She hummed a country song, realizing it was one of Chase's favorites.

Since arriving at the farm, Jas had forgotten all about him. Now she longed for him to be here. Not only did she want to share her happiness with him, but he'd also change the storm from terrifying to an adventure. Plus, now that she'd found Whirlwind, Jas knew for sure there was room in her heart for a cute goof of a guy like Chase. She hoped that when she got back to Virginia, he would still care enough to try again. And this time, she'd put everything into their relationship.

"I can't wait to get you back to Second Chance Farm. I want to introduce you to Miss Hahn, Dr. Danvers, and *Chase*. You'll like him as much as I do. Then there's Shadow. I don't know if you'll like him. He's kind of pushy—"

A sudden bang made her jump. The wind was shaking the left side of the double door so hard, the latch had broken. With a shriek of metal, the door ripped from its track and began flapping like a bird's wing. Rain streamed into the opening.

Jas shuddered. There was no way she could close it. She'd better check to make sure the horses nearest the door were safe.

"Let's visit some of your friends." She led Whirlwind toward the end, stopping in front of the end stall. The wind whistled ominously through the broken door, and rain splattered the aisle floor, but the horse, aside from nerves, appeared okay.

A crash came from the office, then the tinkle of glass, startling Jas. Marietta, belted into her raincoat, flew out the tack room door and down the aisle, punching numbers into her cell phone. "The shutter blew right off the office window," she told Jas. "Rain's pouring in. I'm calling Gerald to report it."

"Tell him the barn door's broken, too. So much for 'hurricane proof.'"

Marietta nodded, her attention on the phone.

"I'll help you get the shutter back up."

"Or at least move furniture and files out of the way so they don't get too soaked." Marietta snapped her phone shut. "No signal. I'm going to drive down the lane to the road and see if I can pick up service."

"In this weather?"

"It's ten feet to the car. Don't worry, if it's too wild, I won't try it." She patted her hair, still smooth after sleeping on the sofa. "After all, I don't want to wreck my makeup *and* my hairdo." She took off again for the tack room.

"Let's make sure the horses are all right and then put you back in the stall," Jas said to Whirlwind. Slowly, she led her down the long aisle, pausing to peer in at each horse. Since the door had blown open, the sounds of the storm had increased in intensity. Some of the horses were weaving, pawing, or bobbing their heads. Jas wished she could go in each stall to calm them with massage. Instead, she stood outside each door, soothing them with words.

"Maybe I can find some hay. Chewing might distract you guys," Jas said when she reached Whirlwind's stall. She turned to lead her into the stall the same time a shadowy figure stepped from it. Jas froze. Lightning crackled overhead. *Hugh.*

A scream of horror rose in her throat. Hugh grabbed the lead line with one hand and Jas's wrist with the other. Before she could react, he hurled her into the stall so hard she slammed into the far wall. Dazed, she gulped air before leaping to her feet. She flew toward the door, but he slammed it shut and bolted it.

"Let me out!" She threw her shoulder against it, but it was built to withstand a thousand pounds of horse, and she bounced off. Falling backward, she landed hard on her side.

Hugh leered at her through the bars. He wore a yellow ascot and tweed jacket as if off to a foxhunting breakfast. "Thank you for being so easy to subdue, Jas," he said, purring the words in his gentleman's voice. His hair and the shoulders of his jacket were wet, as if he'd just run in from the storm.

For a moment, Jas stared at him in disbelief. How had he snuck inside without her seeing him? Then she jumped to her feet. "You horse-murdering—" she spat as she flung herself again at the door. Grabbing the bars, she shook them, repeating, *"Let me out!"*

Hugh made a tsking noise. "All this fuss won't do you any good. I already tested the stall. You're as secure as if you were in a jail cell."

"Where you should be!"

"Oh? And who's going to put me there? You?" His laugh was so smug Jas wanted to spit at him through the bars.

"How did you know I was here?" she spat out instead.

"I always knew where Whirlwind was. It was just a matter of keeping her whereabouts a secret from you—and the insurance company."

"How'd you know we'd found her?" she demanded. "Lucy?"

"Oh, no. Your demise is due to my sweet aunt."

Jas stared at him, not understanding.

"You know, the ever-so-helpful, slightly dotty Mrs. Quincey?"

Jas's stomach dropped. "She spied on me for you?"

"Nothing that dramatic. Aunt Beatrice has a heart of gold, but she also has a tongue easily loosened by a glass of sherry. When she mentioned you were flying to Florida to see your mother, I knew what was really happening."

Jas growled deep in her throat, furious for being so easily duped. Even when she'd told Chase her suspicions about Mrs. Quincey, it had sounded ludicrous.

"It was so sweet when dear Auntie moved to Stanford to live closer to her darling nephew," he went on. "And when she *conveniently* broke her hip, I made sure she recouped in the same nursing home as your grandfather. Then all it took was a little bribe to make sure the two were introduced, and a match was made in heaven." He chuckled nastily. "For me at least."

Jas wanted to strangle Hugh. Instead, she squeezed the bars so hard her fingers hurt. Out of the corner of her eye, she glanced toward the tack room door. If she could keep stalling, Marietta would be . . .

"Don't expect the fearless Detective Baylor to rescue you," Hugh said.

Jas froze. "What did you do to her?"

"I'm afraid she's just had a slight accident."

"Nooo!"

"Hush, Jas. Give it up. There's nothing you can do to save yourself or Whirlwind." Hugh's tone was so condescending and arrogant that goose bumps prickled her arms. She stared unblinkingly at his face, which was shadowed in the dim emergency lights. Yet the evil shone clearly in his eyes.

There was no remorse. No guilt. No glint of sadness at the thought of destroying lives. He'd even used his own aunt to get his way.

I am truly staring into the face of a killer. Jas stumbled away from the door. Whirlwind stood quietly next to Hugh, unaware of what a monster he was. Jas had promised to save her. She'd promised they'd never be apart. *I've failed.*

"Ah, I see from your expression that you realize it's futile to struggle any longer." Hugh's voice was silky smooth. "My plan couldn't have gone better. I have you and Whirlwind right where I want you, Jas. Together, where I can get rid of you both and no one will be the wiser."

Twenty-two

❖　❖　❖

·

JAS'S GAZE FLEW TO WHIRLWIND. "WHAT ARE you going to do with her?" she whispered.

"I don't have to do anything. The storm will do it for me. The hurricane has changed to a category four. How long do you think a pampered show horse can survive in this weather?" His lip curled in a grin. "Ironic, don't you think? Whirlwind will be destroyed by a whirlwind!"

"Don't, Hugh. Please. Don't hurt her."

Hugh sighed. "Too late, Jas. If only you'd heeded my earlier advice to leave well enough alone. Didn't I warn you at the courthouse? None of this would have happened if you'd kept quiet. Whirlwind would have continued to be Early Star, winning ribbons throughout Florida. You'd continue to be a hack rider living at a run-down farm." He adjusted his ascot.

"Unfortunately, you can't seem to comprehend that I will never be prosecuted." With a self-satisfied smile, he turned to lead Whirlwind away. "So be patient, Jas. I'll be back for you in a minute."

"Stop!" Jas hurtled herself at the door. "Don't put her out in the storm, Hugh. Don't you get it? Scott Black is testifying against you. The police know you killed Tommy Looney. So no matter what you do, you won't get away with it!"

"Only, I will, Jas," he said over his shoulder, his words echoing through the barn. "Because people like me *always* win."

Grasping the bars, Jas pressed her cheek against them, trying to see where Hugh was taking the mare. She heard the clank of the sliding barn doors. She heard the whine of the wind and the beating of the rain on the outside of the barn. She heard the slap of the lead line, Hugh's angry voice, and the rattle of the door shutting.

Then Whirlwind was gone.

Frantic, Jas looked around the stall. She had to find a way out. But Hugh was right. The stall was built like a fortress, and it was accident proof, so there was no loose bucket or feed tub to use as a weapon when he came for her. Tilting back her head, she examined the ceiling, hoping to find a hole into the loft. But the ceiling was solid. Like most new barns, the hay was stored separately in case of fire, so there was no hayloft.

Jas was as trapped as the horses. She sank into the shavings, unable to hold back her despair. She couldn't save herself, much less Whirlwind and Marietta.

"Jas?" As if on cue, Marietta appeared at the stall door. Her forehead oozed with blood. Her blond hair was soaked dark red. One eye was swollen shut and the other bruised. Her raincoat was wet with rain or blood or both.

Jas sprang to her feet. "What happened? Are you all right?"

"Car accident," she mumbled, a split in her lip. Her eyes were glazed, and she fumbled at the door latch. Finally she got it open. Jas ran out, catching the investigator before she fell. She helped her to the cot.

"Sit down. You're hurt." Jas glanced fearfully toward the barn door where Hugh had taken Whirlwind. Why hadn't he come back for her? "Hugh's here."

Marietta nodded woozily. "I know. He ran

into my car with his. Felt like I was hit with a tank."

"You need help. There's a first-aid kit in the supply room."

"No." Marietta grabbed Jas to keep her from running off. "I look worse than I am. Really. No broken bones. Just a knocked-in head and bruised vanity. Tell me what happened."

Jas explained in a torrent of words. "He has Whirlwind. We have to go after him."

Marietta stood on shaky legs. She slid her gun from the pocket of her raincoat. Jas grabbed the flashlight off the cot, then zipped her Windbreaker. With Marietta holding on to her arm, the two hurried down the aisle.

When they reached the barn door at the end of the aisle, it took all Jas's strength to open it against the buffeting wind. Clutching each other, they stepped into the pounding rain. Jas was instantly soaked. She shielded her eyes with one hand, trying to see. But as if in a blizzard, the whipping wind and rain created whiteout conditions.

Then a bolt of lightning illuminated a dark mound sprawled about ten feet in front of them. Letting go of Marietta, Jas ran over, struggling against the gusts. She beamed her light on the mound. It was Hugh.

Marietta came up beside her. Kneeling, she felt Hugh's pulse. "He's alive."

Jas crouched beside her. The rain washed blood from an ugly gash on his forehead. "What do you think happened?" she hollered above the noise of the storm.

"Don't know. My guess is Whirlwind panicked. Maybe she reared and struck him with her hoof." Pulling handcuffs from her pocket, she snapped them on his wrists. "Just in case."

Jas shined her light into the dark night. It bounced off a parallel row of white board fence. There was no sign of Whirlwind. Alarm filled her, and she felt feverish despite the chilling rain. "I'm going after her."

Marietta grabbed her wrist. "No. You'll never find her in this weather. And the storm's only getting worse. Help me drag Hugh into the barn."

"I don't care about Hugh." Yanking her arm away, Jas jumped to her feet. She aimed the flashlight onto the gravel. Hoofprints headed down the alley made by the fence. Using the top board as a guide, she followed the trail, her body tipped forward as she sliced through the wind. Branches and leaves were strewn on the grass.

The alley and fence ended at the hay field. Cupping her hands around her mouth, Jas hollered, "Whirlwind!" But the cry couldn't be heard above the howling. A gust slammed her into the board. For a moment, she clung to it. Aiming the beam, she again found Whirlwind's trail. The hoofprints were far apart, as if she'd galloped across the field. Jas shivered, wet to the bone. Should she turn back and wait for help? No, help might take forever to arrive and she'd *promised*.

Jas plunged into the storm. As she ran across the field, the tall grass switched her sodden jeans. "Whirlwind!" she continued to holler, even though she knew it was futile.

The trail disappeared into the woods. Branches snapped as the tops of the pines and oaks whipped back and forth. A limb cracked overhead. Just in time, Jas jumped sideways as it crashed at her feet. She trembled with cold and fatigue. It would be crazy to follow the mare into the woods. Yet, if she didn't, the rain would erase the trail forever.

Desperation pushed Jas into the forest. The beam of her light grew dimmer. Blindly, she made her way from tree to tree. She tripped over logs and roots, her tennis shoes sinking in the saturated earth. Her Windbreaker clung to her body like plastic wrap. Her fingers were stiff with cold.

Suddenly, she realized she'd lost the trail. She swung the light in an arc. Ferns, moss, grassy hummocks, and rocks, but no tracks. Heart thudding, she turned in a circle, searching for an imprint in the leaves or ground. *Nothing.*

Throwing back her head, Jas howled as mournfully as Digger. *"Whirlwind!"* She pictured the mare running headlong into a tree or a ditch. Sobbing, she sank to her knees. Rain pelted her head and flowed under her collar and down her back. The wind threw twigs and dirt in her face. Jas didn't care. Whirlwind was gone.

The mare would never survive a night in a hurricane. Hugh had won after all.

Then a soft whinny came from her right. Startled, Jas whipped her flashlight around, catching the reflection of two eyes and a jagged white star. Whirlwind was walking toward her, dragging a muddy lead line.

With a cry, Jas jumped up and stumbled forward. "It's you!" The mare was dripping wet, bedraggled and shaking. Trembling herself, Jas ran her hands lovingly down Whirlwind's face, neck, ribs, and croup. Her fingers touched sticky wet. She directed the light on the horse's hindquarters, where a deep gash snaked down her flank. It would need stitches and time to heal.

"You'll be okay." Jas kissed the mare's muzzle. Then she began laughing giddily. "You just won't be *perfect* anymore. That means you'll be safe from people like Hugh for the rest of your life." She picked up the dangling rope. "Come on. Let's find our way out of these woods."

Clasping the lead, Jas walked beside Whirlwind, the fingers of her right hand twined in her mane. Somehow, they found their way to the edge of the woods. Through the sheets of rain, Jas saw a light bobbing across the field. She heard Marietta's voice, faint in the thunder of the hurricane.

Side by side, Jas and Whirlwind made their

way toward the light. The wind lashed Jas's shoulders like a whip. The rain swirled her hair and tore at her arms.

She tightened her grip on the mare's mane. *Let the storm rage,* Jas thought. She wasn't letting go of her beloved horse. *Ever.*